Over the Joshua Slope

by Lyman Hafen

BRADBURY PRESS
NEW YORK

Maxwell Macmillan Canada
Toronto

Maxwell Macmillan International
New York   Oxford   Singapore   Sydney

For my father and friend,
Kelton Hafen

"A Boy Named Sue" Words and music by Shel Silverstein copyright © 1969, Evil Eye Music, Inc., Daytona Beach, Florida. Used by permission.

Bradbury Press
Macmillan Publishing Company
866 Third Avenue
New York, NY 10022

Maxwell Macmillan Canada, Inc.
1200 Eglinton Avenue East
Suite 200
Don Mills, Ontario M3C 3N1

Macmillan Publishing Company is part of the Maxwell Communication Group of Companies.

First edition
Printed and bound in the United States of America

10   9   8   7   6   5   4   3   2   1

The text of this book is set in ITC New Baskerville.

Library of Congress Cataloging-in-Publication Data
Hafen, Lyman.
Over the Joshua Slope / by Lyman Hafen.—1st ed.
p.   cm.
Summary: When twelve-year-old Brian Winsor accompanies his stern father and two other seasoned cowboys on his first cattle drive, he learns a lot about life as well as herding cattle.
ISBN 0-02-741100-1
[1. Fathers and sons—Fiction.   2. Cattle drives—Fiction.   3. Cowboys—Fiction.]   I. Title.
PZ7.H1197Ov   1994
[Fic]—dc20   93-30712

. . . for ye have not passed this way heretofore.

Joshua 3:4

1

◀◀◀○▶▶▶

My father wrestled his truck through another rut. The steering wheel fought back like a worthy opponent, jerking and twisting against his sturdy grip. "There she sits," Dad said, "big and pretty." He looked north across the humps and hollows of a gray desert that rose toward the purple folds of a mountain in the distance.

"The Joshua Slope?" I asked.

Just then the truck bounded out of another gash in the road. I sprang off the seat and collided with the top of the cab. The crown of my cowboy hat collapsed like an accordion and for an instant I was far away. Then I heard my father's voice again.

"The county grader," he answered. He cocked his head to the right and pointed with his chin. "Sitting there big and pretty, and about as much help as a pile of scrap metal."

I drew my eyes back from the broad scene before me and focused them on a bright yellow road grader with gleaming black tires parked in the brush fifty feet off the road. It looked like a giant insect from another world. We roared by and left the lonesome machine in a curling cloud of dust.

"Your tax dollars at work," Dad grumbled. Disgust shot down through his crippled leg, directly to his foot on the gas pedal. He gunned the gas so hard my head slammed against the back of the cab. Now the brim of my hat was bent, as well. "They spend half the county budget on a fine piece of equipment to keep these washboarded ruts halfway smooth, then they park the thing out here like some kind of monument. Meanwhile, we're expected to negotiate the most godforsaken road on the planet."

The next stretch of that cursed dirt road looked almost smooth to me. It seemed safe now; I took off my hat and pulled it back into shape. Dad glanced over at me. As soon as he saw my hatless head, he swung his eyes quickly away. "Thought you were gonna get that hair cut," he growled.

"I did," I said.

"Thought you were gonna get a *real* haircut this time."

Dad eventually dragged his eyes back to me and examined my head the same way he studied the build of a newborn colt. My face grew warm, then hot with embarrassment. I jammed my hat back on and looked out the window to my right. "It's just a razor cut," I finally said. "All the guys at school have one." The sagebrush whizzed by in a blur and after a long silence I looked over at Dad, whose eyes seemed lost somewhere out on the desert. He said nothing more about my haircut. Silence was his response, and it said more than words.

It was hot in the truck. My sweaty back stuck to the vinyl seat and made a funny sucking sound every time I leaned forward. Dad, who was never one for extras, had opted for a radio in his new cattle truck, but had declined on an air conditioner. The air whistling through the open windows of the cab must have been pushing ninety degrees.

That was because it was almost summer. The summer I would turn thirteen.

Dad had managed to get me excused from the last week of school so I could help him round up cows on the Joshua Slope. Once they were gathered, we would trail the cattle up to summer pasture on Clover Mountain. For me it was like living a dream—a week out of school, and not sick or anything.

I couldn't believe I was there, right there on the front seat of my father's two-ton GMC cattle truck. We were already twenty-five miles out of town, having turned off the paved highway ten miles back. Now it was a roller-coaster ride on a one-lane dirt road from hell. I clung to the armrest on the door and bounced like a basketball as Dad cussed every wretched bump. He winced each time we hit a rough spot because his right knee had a heavy brace strapped to it and he was in about as much pain as a man can stand. That's why I was out of school. Dad needed me for legs.

"This will be no vacation," Dad reminded me as we moved farther from town and deeper into the desert.

"I know that," I said, though I knew nothing of what lay ahead.

There came another long silence, which is how it

had been all morning—a short piece of talk followed by a long space of quiet. Dad was never the kind to take a stick to a kid, but he could punish you soundly with silence.

Two horses, Justice and Buck, rode in the back of the truck. I could see their smooth, muscled chests through the rear window of the cab, their legs spread wide and their shoulders braced against the stock racks, taking the wild ride in stride. The bouncing and bumping were routine for the horses, part of their job. All of our gear was wrapped in a huge canvas tarp and strapped securely to a rack above the cab.

We had been late leaving town that morning because I had to stop by the school and hand in my final state history assignment. It was a research paper on Paiute Indian legends. I had delivered it to Mr. Mulligan just before the bell for first period.

"Aren't you forgetting something?" Mr. Mulligan had groaned as I hurried off. He was a walrus of a man, huge and flabby, and even a short sentence like that ran him out of breath. I turned and he handed back the report. "To whom do I credit the A if your name is not on it?"

I grabbed the report, pleased that Mr. Mulligan

expected me to score so high, and scrawled "Brian Winsor" at the top of the first page. On the way out I nearly collided with Michael Bonner. "Thought you was out of here," he said. My best friend, Michael Bonner was about a head taller than me. He had on stone-washed denim shorts that came to his knees and a U2 T-shirt. His books were slung over his shoulder in a backpack.

"I *am* out of here," I said. "In fact, you could say I'm history."

"Sure you don't want to borrow my Walkman?" Michael asked. I had spent half of the night before at Michael's house listening to music.

"Not this time," I said. "I've got to start thinking like a cowboy."

Michael socked me in the shoulder as I started down the hall. "Don't go punching any dogies," he said. The only thing Michael Bonner knew about cowboys was what he saw on "Bonanza" reruns on cable TV. He swung his backpack around his head and let out a "Woopie-ti-yi-yay."

By now a bunch of other guys had stopped in the hall. They all started singing the theme from "Bonanza": "Dum da-da dum da-da dum da-da dum da-da DUMM-DUMM."

"See you at the Ponderosa," one of them crowed as I ducked through the exit door.

Now we were headed for the Slope, Dad and I. We drove headlong into the desert. Before us rolled a desperate country: crusty slopes, winding dry washes, and tall, shaggy Joshua trees everywhere you looked. It was an old and tired landscape, the kind of place most people would give up for dead.

"Are we on the Slope yet?" I asked Dad after another long silence.

"Depends on what you call the Slope," he said.

"The Joshua Slope," I said. "Where does it start?"

"Right here if you want it to," Dad answered. He looked straight on, his jaw set like concrete.

"Isn't there a map?" I asked. "Isn't there some kind of boundary, like a state line?"

"The Slope is the Slope," Dad said. "You can draw lines on a map till the cows come home. The Slope will still be the Slope. You'll know it when you're there."

I had never been to the Joshua Slope. I knew it only through stories. The Joshua Slope was my father's winter range. He owned grazing rights on it and paid fees to the Bureau of Land Management to use it, just as my Grandpa Winsor had. Dad said cattle ranged that country as far as the eye could see. I took him at his word because I could not see any cows. He said on a desert like this, with all its gullies and gulches, you would see cows only on occasion, or if you knew exactly where to look for them.

I watched my father as he jockeyed the truck down the ragged road. The same bumps that tossed me to the roof of the cab hardly displaced him. He rode the truck the way he used to ride a horse, as if he were born there. His sweat-soiled hat was tipped back on his head and his dark eyes burned with a solitary bitterness. His long shirt sleeves were rolled up almost to his elbows and his knotted hands clenched the steering wheel like vise grips, never giving way, even when the wheel wanted to spin back fast. He looked like he was exactly where he belonged, with one foot always in the future. He seemed to be one thought, one step, one movement ahead of everything. I felt completely the opposite, like I didn't belong at all. What's more, I had no idea where I *did* belong. I wanted to see a map and know where things started and where they ended, and where I was supposed to fit in all of it.

I glanced at the brace on my father's leg and shamefully turned my eyes away.

2

◄◄◄○►►►

Most of the time I could see the top of the country all the way to the mountain. It was reassuring to have everything in sight, all of it in one sweep. Then we would drop into a dry wash and the world would shrink to the distance between one ledge and another. Before I knew it, we were out on high ground again, and I'd feel that confidence once more, that satisfaction of having it all before me.

Then we came to a place where the earth fell out from under us. My stomach rose in my chest as the road suddenly cut down a steep ledge and the truck began to descend, like a zigzagging bird, to the floor of a deep, broad canyon. An eroded sandstone cliff on the far side of the gorge looked like it might have once been the face of the Great Sphinx. As we carefully made our way down the ridge, I imagined I was in Egypt, the country my fellow seventh graders were studying in geography that morning. Dad seemed to be in some kind of trance. His eyes were fixed like lasers on the road as he maneuvered the truck through the switchbacks, pulling sharply around one turn, then deliberately lining up his approach for the next.

I waited until we were nearly to the bottom before I finally spoke. "So anyway," I said, "what do they call this canyon?"

"Beaver Creek," Dad answered. He frowned at me as he said it, as if I had asked a dumb question, as if anyone with any brains at all would know that this was Beaver Creek Canyon.

Along the bottom of the gorge the road cut through a thick stand of cottonwood trees, one of the few patches of green I had seen all morning, and crossed the meager flow of the creek. There was no need for a bridge here. We simply drove through the stream as it lapped softly at the wheels of the truck. Then we began the climb up the other side.

"So anyway," I ventured again, "what do cows eat out here all winter?" I knew Dad would talk if the subject was cattle.

"Plenty," Dad answered without taking his eyes off the road. "Plenty, if it rains. If it don't rain, they go hungry. It rains and the cicardy and the bunchgrass come out like a blessing. Green and lush. Just like ice-cream dessert. It don't rain and they make do on blackbrush."

"Looks like it hardly ever rains out here," I said.

"Good thing we got plenty of blackbrush," Dad said.

I thought back to when I was younger—when Dad and I had been very close, like good friends. He had taught me to ride and help take care of the horses, and how to handle cattle. We had done all of that at the homestead up on Clover Mountain where we spent two weeks every summer, or in town at our feedyard out on the edge of the last neighborhood. This was the first time he had brought me to the Joshua Slope. He had put off bringing me here until he thought I was ready. And even now he didn't seem to think I was ready, but he needed my legs, so there wasn't a choice.

When I was younger, my father had always told me stories, fine stories of the range and of old cowboys like my Grandpa Winsor, who died when I was just a baby. He told me tales about how they camped on the desert for weeks at a time and ate nothing but beef jerky and beans. Dad didn't tell me stories anymore. Now I was beginning to realize how much I missed them.

A few miles beyond Beaver Creek we came to a fence and crossed a cattle guard.

"Now you're in Nevada," Dad said. We worked our way northward along the rim of a deep dry wash. "That's the Bull Valley Wash," Dad said. "Runs into Beaver Creek." We seemed to be climbing now, slowly pulling higher. The country sloped upward to the foot of a mountain on the horizon. I was reasonably sure that the mountain in the distance was Clover Mountain—sure enough, at least, to not risk asking another dumb question.

I studied the landscape and began to see its patterns. Countless shadowed draws broke out of the long ridges, cut down in V shapes, and ended in the bottoms of winding dry washes that were as wide as a road. The draws had all been cut by cloudbursts, I figured, those rare storms each year when water ran in torrents and flooded south, everything rolling and tumbling southward down the Slope.

We drove on toward the Upper Well, which Dad told me would be our first camp. He assured me the Upper Well was just beyond the sharp-tipped ridge that I could now see standing like a pyramid just a few miles distant. "That's Signal Peak," he said.

Then, as the truck chugged to the top of another rise, the entire scene suddenly changed. The sun ducked behind a feathery cloud and there was a new, subdued light across the landscape. Everything looked more defined now, more immediate and real—and I knew then that we were on the Joshua Slope. It rolled out before us like a wrinkled rug dotted with Joshua trees, and stretched all the way up to where the mountain stood like a promise on the skyline.

Wherever the line was, I knew we had crossed it. I felt something strong and final, as if a door had closed behind me. There was nothing left now but to cross the Slope.

Dad had the radio on. It was turned down low so all you heard was static. We were pulling higher now and the signal began to strengthen, and Dad turned the knob just enough to catch some music. I held my breath as he dialed in the song. It was a rap tune. As soon as the beat registered on Dad, he clicked it off.

I let out a discouraged breath.

More than anything I wanted to reach over and turn the radio back on. I wanted to crank it up high and let it blow the doors off. I might as well have wished for a big-screen TV mounted on the hood of the truck with MTV blasting from the speakers. It would never happen. Not as long as Dad was any- where within hearing distance. Not on the Slope.

3

◀◀◀○▶▶▶

It was midmorning when we reached the ridge above camp. From there the Upper Well looked like nothing more than a clump of green at the bottom of a gray canyon. Dad took the truck slowly down the last leg of steep road into camp. He backed up to a sandbank that was even with the tailgate and we got out and unloaded the horses. Dad handed me both lead ropes and instructed me to put Buck and Justice in the corral over by the windmill, and to toss them each a flake of crisp green alfalfa hay from the stack next to the fence.

A hot wind huffed down the canyon. It was a whipping wind that coughed and spit and quit, then started up again. As I led the horses over to the corral, the wind ripped my hat off and sent it spinning across the sand. I dropped the lead ropes and took off chasing the hat until it lodged against the trunk of a Joshua tree. Meanwhile, Buck took off trotting up the road as if he was headed back to town. I hustled around the horse and headed him off before the idea completely took hold of him. It was just like Buck to do that. Seemed like there was a problem following him everywhere he went. I gave the lead rope a hard jerk to let him know I wasn't pleased. Justice, on the other hand, had wandered up to the haystack and was chomping a mouthful of hay, just waiting like a good servant. By the time I finished taking care of the horses, I realized it had taken me ten minutes to do a job my father would have finished in seconds.

Two other cattle trucks with bright red stock racks were parked among the rocks and creosote at the Upper Well. On the other side of the windmill, two men who looked a lot older than my father sat in tattered lawn chairs near a fire. The fire was obviously not built for warmth, but to brew the coffee they were sipping. I could hear them talking. They greeted Dad as he hobbled up, jabbing him about the monstrous brace on his leg and his showing up so late.

"When you bring the boy along, things don't move so fast," Dad told them. I trudged over to the fire and, not knowing what to do with myself, stopped a few steps behind Dad. Suddenly I realized how silly I looked. The men all wore boots that looked like they had ten thousand miles on them, crusty Levi's, and faded shirts. I had on a crisp new blue-denim pair of Wranglers that came down perfectly creased over shiny boots, and a bright new plaid shirt that Mom had bought me specially for the cattle drive.

The two strangers looked at me now. Dad turned toward me, grinning, and said, "He's the best help I could scare up." The old cowboys chuckled and sized me up. I felt like a horse on exhibit in the auction ring. One, the man named Malcolm Higginbotham, had a fairly grumpy look on his face. He appeared to me to be eighty years old, though I learned later he was only sixty-five. A short, crumpled cigarette dangled from his cracked lips and he nothing more than grunted at me as a greeting.

The other man, whose name was Will Buchanan, seemed much more pleasant. The first time he looked at me, his eyes seemed to light up beneath his dark glasses. He smiled wide, so wide I saw the gold caps on two of his upper teeth. The sun glinted off those gold teeth and I felt something good run through me. From that first moment things seemed right between Will and me. I could tell he was willing to give me the benefit of the doubt, take me at face value—innocent until proven guilty.

"What's your name, son?" Will asked. His voice was soft like a whisper, but it had an unusual rough edge to it.

"Brian," I replied.

"Brian Winsor," Will said. "Jake Winsor's number one son. If you're Jacob's boy, you're okay in my book. Welcome to the Joshua Slope, young man. You're the only body on the whole outfit that's got legs with any spring left in 'em." I was taken aback by Will's soft-rough voice. It reminded me of Rod Stewart, one of my favorite rock singers, and I chuckled inside at the thought of Will Buchanan singing on a music video. It hadn't occurred to me yet that Will's unique voice was probably the result of a lifetime of hollering at cows.

I looked over at Malcolm Higginbotham, who sat with his legs crossed and his eyes focused on the ground. He grumbled something to the effect that it would take more than a little spring in the legs to get this herd gathered.

The three men spent the rest of the morning planning. They talked of places I'd heard of but had never seen, like the Burn and Salt Pond and Cedar Wash and Dodge Spring. I wandered around camp, tossing rocks and chasing lizards while they drew plans in the dirt. I investigated the entire compound they called the Upper Well. It sat beneath two tall, rocky ridges, and it seemed a colorless place, painted only by varying shades of gray.

A short way from the fire stood a tall, silver windmill, its blades whistling in the wind that snaked down the canyon. The windmill's shaft thunked up and down, hefting precious water from deep in the gray earth and pushing it out through a narrow pipe into a huge round trough. A large maze of corrals surrounded the trough. They were stockade corrals—one gray cedar post set against another, tight as a braid, forming what looked to me like a solid barrier against even the wildest cow on the Joshua Slope. A few cottonwood trees and willow bushes grew around the wet perimeter of the water hole.

Up on a small rise stood a dilapidated clapboard

shack, maybe ten feet by twelve feet—a one-room affair with a bunk bed and cookstove in it. Fifty feet beyond the shack was an outhouse made of warped and weathered pine boards. It was a one-seater with just enough room to sit down. Looking at the outhouse reminded me of the time Dad told me how the Upper Well actually had the largest bathroom in the world. "Big as all outdoors," he had said with a silly grin. That was in the days when we were close, back when he told me stories.

There were rocks everywhere—sharp, jagged rocks along the ledges above, and smooth, rounded rocks across the flat wash bottom. Kicking around in the dry sand, I got a closer look at the rocks. I reached down and picked up a smoothly polished stone. Rolling it in my fingers, I discovered there really was some color here. Locked in the rock were swirling patterns of pink, yellow, red, and even blue. Suddenly I realized that all the rocks had a trace of color if you looked at them up close, yet the landscape itself seemed nothing more than gray.

After my inspection tour I slipped over to the fire, squatted next to Dad, and listened. Between the three of them these cowboys had about three hundred head of cows to gather, and most every cow would have a tiny calf born that spring tagging along-side. The cattle were spread over more than twenty square miles. I listened closely and learned that most of the cows and calves would be picked up at watering holes, but some would have to be flushed out of the draws and thickets as far away as Dodge Spring.

The three men were completely caught up in their business. They churned and plowed the ground around the fire, drawing lines and arrows and circles with sticks. I knew a little about how their operations worked. I knew they each owned about a third of the cattle that ranged in common on the Slope. Late each May the cows were gathered, most of them with their young calves, some of them heavy and ready to give birth, and driven twenty miles up the Slope through Bunker Pass and all the way to the meadows on Clover Mountain for the summer. In the fall the calves were weaned, fed up, and sold—except for a few of the very best females, which were kept as re-placement heifers for the oldest cows. Then, in mid-October, the cows were trailed back down the Slope for another winter. It was a continuous circle that my father, Malcolm Higginbotham, Will Buchanan, and their fathers before them had been making for nearly a century.

I watched Will Buchanan through all the ceremony of planning. I noticed he was a good listener. He seldom opened his mouth, but when he did, the others listened closely because Will did not waste words. I also noticed that Will often looked over at a golden palomino tied to his truck. The horse looked very well-bred to me. He was built just the way my dad liked a horse: short on top and long underneath, with a lot of bunchy muscle in the shoulders and hindquarters—pretty head, too. I knew enough about horses to be certain he was a quarter horse. And I could tell Will was proud of the animal just by the way he looked at him.

"Grab the ice chest, Brian," Dad said when the planning session finally ended. I pulled a large metal chest out of the truck and lugged it over to the fire. Dad fixed up a pile of cold-cut sandwiches and pulled open a bag of potato chips. We tore into the food like lions. The sandwiches, smothered in mayonnaise, tasted magnificent. I ate three of them, chasing everything down with a frosty can of root beer. Dad poured a bag of cookies onto the camp table for dessert. I ate a handful of cookies and filled my shirt pockets with five or six more.

4

◀◀◀○▶▶▶

After lunch Dad told me to saddle Justice. I went to the corral and haltered the big sorrel gelding. Buck, a smaller black horse, tried to follow us out of the corral. I quickly shut the gate and cut him off. "Back off, you miserable crow-bait," I growled at Buck. "You're not going anywhere." Why Dad had brought Buck along was a mystery to me. I certainly didn't plan on riding him. I led Justice over to the truck, where we had unloaded the saddles and all the rest of the gear. He cocked a hind leg, relaxed, and nearly went to sleep while I brushed him.

"You'll be riding with Malcolm this afternoon," Dad informed me as I curried the dust off Justice's muscled red shoulders.

My heart sank at the news. I had hoped to ride with Will, and I figured Dad knew as much. Why was he sending me off with the old grouch?

"Ride beside him," Dad said, "not behind him. You'll be gathering all the stock hanging around Salt Pond. Listen close to Malcolm and do as he says."

I hefted my saddle onto Justice's back and swung around to the off side to straighten the cinches. "What about Will?" I asked. "Couldn't I ride with him?"

"Will's gonna make a circle up around the Burn. He can cover that himself. Malcolm will need help out at the pond."

Dad stood with all his weight on his left leg. The metal brace strapped to his right knee looked as foreign on him as a suit and tie would have looked. Not until that moment did I think of how hard it must have been for my father not to be able to ride. I knew he lived for days like this. But now he was grounded, stuck in camp as chief cook and bottle washer. He couldn't as much as swing his leg over the saddle, and even if he could, the pain of riding would be ten times greater than the disappointment of staying in camp.

*   *   *

My watch showed two o'clock straight up as Malcolm and I rode out from the Upper Well. The wind died down as our horses plodded up a cow trail to the top of the ridge. When we topped out and started across the country there was nothing but the Joshua Slope before us and the dry, mellow smell of blackbrush.

Malcolm, a small hunch of a man, sat atop a long gray mare he called Witch. The mare's mane was scraggly and I wondered why he didn't comb it. I was too self-concerned at the time to realize that Malcolm had arthritic shoulders and probably couldn't reach that high. I rode alongside Malcolm for a while, but Witch stepped out smartly and Justice was never known as a walker. To keep up I had to push Justice at a teeth-rattling trot, which grew old quickly, so I let him settle into his slow amble and fell behind a couple of lengths. From my rear position I watched every move Malcolm made, but could not see the expressions on his face. I wondered what the old man was thinking and imagined that he was probably scheming some plan to ditch me.

Once in a while Malcolm would turn slowly in the saddle and bend his head around to check on me. Each time he seemed almost surprised that I was still

25

there. He didn't say anything the first mile or so. Later, as he lit a cigarette, he turned and motioned for me to catch up. I kicked Justice in the ribs and trotted up alongside the old man.

"You know this country at all?" Malcolm asked.

"Just from stories," I said.

"You'll never learn it sittin' back there daydreaming—gawking at this mare's hind end all day."

That was all he said. I assumed he meant I should ride alongside him and watch the country. Which I did for a while, but it soon turned into an ordeal— riding next to the grouchy old troll, wondering whether to say something and, if so, what. Justice lagged behind again and I was content to let him drift. I felt more comfortable looking at Witch's rear end than trying to keep my position next to Ebenezer Scrooge.

From behind I continued to size up old Malcolm. He had on a funky-looking brown felt hat, a strange cross between a cowboy hat and the kind of hat a gangster would wear in a movie. His shirt was one of those beige work shirts like a guy might wear on a loading dock. He had on the most wrinkled pair of soiled Levi's I'd ever seen, and, to beat all, he didn't even wear cowboy boots. Instead, he had on an oily pair of lace-up work boots like the guy on the loading dock would also be wearing. Old Malcolm sat up on Witch like a little monkey on a big football, and he savored his cigarette as if it might be the last one he'd ever get to smoke.

Justice carried me up one ridge and down another. He clinked across the rocky ground at an easy, lumbering pace. Time labored by like the landscape, slowly enough for my mind to rush ahead and circle back and loiter in the space between here and there. I began to hum songs from my CD collection.

Malcolm finally looked around. "How old are you, son?" He spoke without taking the cigarette from his mouth.

"Twelve, going on thirteen," I said. "I turn thirteen next month."

"Yeah," Malcolm growled, "figured you was about that. Sheesh, when I was your age, I was tendin' sheep alone, six weeks at a time, out on Black Rock."

I wasn't in the mood for one of those "When-I-was-your-age" stories. Fortunately, Malcolm didn't go into detail.

We rode through the Joshua trees, wove through them like thread. Most of the trees stood as tall as my horse, some much taller, some shorter. They were scattered at random across the country and they reminded me of a set of plastic cowboy figures I had when I was a little kid, good guys and outlaws I'd set up across the living room carpet—clustered here and there, each one in a different pose. Each one a different man. The green, swordlike leaves of the Joshua were flat and sharp, and the dark brown bark on the trunks was cracked and broken into flakes. I wondered why they called them Joshua trees.

Malcolm would know, I figured. He'd know why they called these weird-looking trees Joshuas. It took me a while to work up the nerve to ask.

"Pioneers named 'em that," Malcolm said when I finally asked. He turned in his saddle and looked back at me, cigarette dangling between his lips. "A century ago when the pioneers first crossed this slope, they thought these trees looked like old Joshua himself with his arms raised—pointing them on toward the promised land. Showin' 'em the way across—the way to whatever it was they were looking for."

It sounded like a good answer to me, but old Malcolm wasn't finished. He was apparently some kind of authority on the Joshua tree. "They only live on slopes like this. You get any higher or any lower and they disappear. The older son of mine—he's a range

28

scientist—says these trees live only where there's hot summers and cold winters. They pretty much die in the winter. They need that. Then they come back in the summer, flower out in the early spring and come back to life in the heat of the year."

Malcolm rode along with his chin in the air, urging Witch through the brush—the proud little grouchy professor. "Hell, some o' these trees is three hundred years old," he added. "There's trees here that was standing when Washington wrote the Declaration of Independence."

"I believe that was Jefferson," I said.

Malcolm looked at me, embarrassed. I had crossed him on a point of history and it was obvious he didn't appreciate it. "Jefferson, Washington, one of those wood-toothed powder-heads," Malcolm said. "They was odd-lookin' fellers," he went on, "but I'll tell ya, they were men. We could use a few of 'em right now in this day and age. Whole country's goin' down the wash fast. Ain't no real men left."

I smiled at all this. Then I started to chuckle. Malcolm came across to me like a funny little cartoon character. One of those Looney Tune fellows with a snively voice that makes you laugh, but all the time you know he's figuring out some way to run you off a cliff, or blow you up, or slam you into a wall. I chuckled, but suddenly I realized Malcolm was serious. I stopped chuckling when it dawned on me that Malcolm didn't appreciate it.

Justice and I fell back again. I kept close watch of Malcolm. His mannerisms intrigued me, the way he lifted his hat and rubbed his forehead with the sleeve of his shirt, and his constant flicking of the cigarette with his arm fully extended to the side. Once I noticed him stick his finger into his ear and turn it back and forth. Then he dabbed the finger on his lips. From the corner of his eye he must have seen me watching, and must have noticed my eyes bulge in disbelief. He smiled and turned in the saddle.

"Natural lip protection," he said. "If you don't lick 'em, they won't chap."

"But . . ."

Malcolm's face turned serious and he said, "Don't knock it. It works."

I nodded as if he made sense. Then we rode on in silence.

On the horizon, silhouetted before the chalky blue sky, I noticed three elderly Joshua trees. They stood bent and tangled like old men, each one pointing up toward the promised land.

5

◀◀◀○▶▶▶

The trouble with Signal Peak was that it looked about the same from any angle. It was the only distinct landmark on the entire up-and-down desert called the Joshua Slope. Its thin ridge muscled high out of the broken landscape and stood like an ancient temple against the sky. Still, after an hour of riding, Signal Peak looked the same to me as it did when we left the Upper Well.

Two hours out of camp Malcolm and I topped the ridge overlooking Salt Pond and finally saw some cattle. At least a dozen cows, each with a springy little calf nearby, stood along the pond bank. They were fat, slick cows—most of them red with white bolly faces, a couple of them coal black with white patches on their foreheads. Salt Pond was a small, muddy water hole fed by a trickling stream that meandered down from the north. The pond was about the size of a basketball court and there were dozens of salt blocks set out around it. The blocks were one-foot cubes of shiny rock salt that my father and the others had packed out on horseback the previous fall. Each block was covered with polished, rounded indentations where the cows had licked.

As we headed down the ridge, the cows began to turn and waddle away. The calves hopped and bucked and shot into the brush. I nudged Justice with the idea of going after them, but pulled back at the sound of Malcolm's voice. "Leave 'em be," he said. "We'll pick 'em up on the way back."

I was disappointed. Since we'd left camp, I'd been straining my eyes looking for cows, and now that we'd found some, I was expected to just ignore them.

Malcolm rode a few more steps toward the pond, then stopped and swung out of the saddle. He squatted, flipped his cigarette away, picked up a stick, and began to draw a map of the general area in the dirt.

"Here's the situation," Malcolm said. He grunted, shifted on his haunches, and rubbed the gray stubble on his chin. "You ride due west, all the way out to this bald knoll." I studied the lines and circles in the dirt, then looked up at the desert and tried to equate the map with the landscape. I didn't have a clue which direction was west, or the presence of mind to look up and see which way the sun was dipping. I should have asked him then, should have admitted to Malcolm that I was as green as a juniper tree. But I let it slip and once that first chance passed, it became more and more difficult to reveal how little I knew. Pride had caught me in its trap.

"Check all the draws as you go," Malcolm said. "Gather anything you come across. Just take 'em with you and move on. Circle fairly wide around the knoll and swing north a piece before you start back. We'll pick up the cattle here at water when we get back."

Malcolm lit another cigarette. The dirt around him had been plowed into a curious jumble of lines and dots and Xs. I looked down at the ground and back up at the landscape. For me the map was no closer to reality than the complicated equations Mr. Cox scratched on the board every morning in second period algebra. Still, I didn't ask any questions. I let my pride convince me that I could figure it out. West, I began to believe, was off to my right. And that hump out in the distance had to be the bald knoll.

"I'm going east and then south," Malcolm said. He cut a big arc in the dirt with his stick. "I'll make my own circle and meet you right here in two hours. That'll give us just enough daylight to make camp before dark."

Malcolm rose slowly from his squatting position and I could almost hear his knees creak. He tossed his drawing stick into the pond and a gust of wind pushed it far out into the water. When I looked down at the ground for one last view of the map, it was gone. The wind had blown it away and all that remained was the land itself.

At first the idea of riding alone terrified me. A blunt prong of fear pushed through my chest. The anxiety eased as I realized that all I had to do now was watch Malcolm go east, then ride in the opposite direction. I began to feel more confident, and then, suddenly, I liked the idea of being rid of Malcolm for a while.

When I looked over at Malcolm, his beady little eyes were locked on mine, awaiting my response. It hit me then that Malcolm might have been setting me up for something. Maybe he had been vague and quick on purpose just so I would have to chicken out and say no. Maybe that was what he was up to—just trying to make me squirm.

If he was bluffing, I wasn't going to let him get away with it.

"Okay," I said. "Meet you back here in two hours."

Malcolm shook his head as if in disgust of my entire generation. He led Witch over to a large rock and stood her next to it, then stepped up on the rock and slowly hoisted himself onto the saddle. I threw the reins over Justice's shoulders and hopped into the stirrups in one quick, clean jump.

Malcolm was watching me again when I looked up from straightening my reins. His eyes were hard and glazed; there was no expression in them. He jerked both arms to the right, jarring the bit in Witch's mouth, and turned the old gray mare in her tracks. I nudged Justice with the heels of my boots and turned him the other way.

More than anything I wanted to find cattle, large bunches of cows and calves. I wanted to find them and gather them into a tight group, a sizable herd that would impress Malcolm. I rode into the afternoon with great expectations and with my eyes glued to the landscape, searching every draw, every gully, every ridgetop. With my hopes running high, time moved quickly at first. After a while, though, that hope began to spread thin and time slowed down as the prospect of finding any cattle started to dim. If there was anything at all along that stretch, any life beyond flashing lizards and buzzing flies, I didn't see it. I saw nothing but gray rock, creosote, blackbrush, and Joshua trees. No cows. No cows anywhere.

It suddenly occurred to me that maybe Malcolm had sent me this way on purpose, turned me loose on a wild-goose chase. He was probably chuckling his way across the country right then, picking up cattle at every turn, knowing all the while that there weren't any cows out around the bald knoll.

The bald knoll. Where was the bald knoll? I'd been looking so hard for cattle, I'd lost sight of my reference point. Now it was gone. The bald knoll had mysteriously disappeared.

I dropped into another dry wash and rode up the ridge on the other side. The landscape looked different now. Everything looked different. I thought about what Dad had said about riding alongside Malcolm and what Malcolm had said about watching the country. There had been no need to study the country as long as I was riding behind Malcolm. Witch's rear end had been the only reference point I needed. Now the entire Slope spread out like a mystery before me. I could turn and look behind me and see Signal Peak on the horizon, which gave my heart a boost, but the bald knoll had simply disappeared.

I rode further into that puzzling territory, deeper into the afternoon. The sun began to fall in the sky before me. *The sun always sets in the west*, I told myself. *At least I'm heading west.*

The minutes quickly mounted to an hour, then two. Before I knew it, my watch was pushing six o'clock. My mind told me I should turn back—I could backtrack quickly now and get to the pond where Malcolm was probably waiting—but my heart pushed me on. After all, I had no cattle. My pride would not allow me to return to the pond without cattle. Justice and I wandered now with no point on the landscape to ride to, clinging only to some frayed little thread of hope that there might be a stray cow out here somewhere.

Late afternoon began to draw heavily around me. The only sound was the constant chinking of Justice's hooves against the rocks. When I stopped him once to look around, the silence settled on my shoulders like barbells in the weight room at school. Justice stood dead still, his ears pricked forward as if he could hear something. I turned in the saddle and drank in the landscape all the way around me. Then came a whooshing from above—air whistling through wings—and I looked up as a lone black crow flew calmly over, flapping its wings, then glided off toward the sun. I wished for a moment that I was the crow and could soar into the sky and see everything. I would fly to the top of Signal Peak and get my bearings, see where everything lay in relationship to everything else. Then I would swoop down, air singing under my wings, locate all the cattle, and push them proudly back to Salt Pond.

I convinced myself to keep riding, to keep looking for the bald knoll, to keep searching for cows and calves. I would prove Malcolm wrong and find some cattle out here even if he didn't think there were any. I would make my circle and return with some kind of honor. In the meantime, the sun kept tumbling toward the horizon. I didn't watch it with my eyes, but my heart could feel it falling.

Another hour passed and there was no bald knoll. My feet had grown tingly and numb in the stirrups and my back ached as if I'd been shot from behind by an arrow. Now my mind began to play games. I imagined I was actually *on* the bald knoll at that very moment and didn't even know it. Maybe the bald knoll was beneath me and was so big that I could ride for hours and not get across it, or around it, much less see it. My chest filled with panic and I suddenly decided to turn Justice back toward Signal Peak. We turned in one quick motion and headed toward the peak until I realized that we were not backtracking at all, but were now in completely new country. I began to turn Justice right and left. We tried one direction for a few minutes, then another. The sun was in a free fall now. It would set within an hour. The day was slipping away and I knew Malcolm would be at the pond by now, would have been there long by now—waiting and smoking and swearing. I could not admit the truth—not yet. But at a certain point in the next hour, somewhere in the soft, late light, I completely forgot about the cattle, forgot about the bald knoll, forgot about returning with honor, and finally let the chill move into my heart.

Somewhere in the lengthening shadows of evening I finally admitted that I was lost.

6

◄◄◄○►►►

It was the first time I remembered being truly alone. Yet it was not so much being alone that frightened me, but much more the stark fact that I didn't know where I was.

I held the reins tight in my fists, so tight my knuckles froze in a locked position. I forced Justice away from the falling sun, thinking that had to be the way we must go. He kept pulling to the left and I forced him to go the way I thought he should—away from the sunset and into the shadows. I no longer watched the landscape, but craned my neck and looked at the ground with a desperate hope of picking up our tracks. I studied every square foot of earth that passed below us. The ground was thick with rocks and even if there had been tracks, the shadows had grown too dark to see them.

There was only Signal Peak now. It stood tall, sharp, and black against the gray sky. Its profile looked no different now than it had when I left the pond.

The sun's afterglow filtered over the far western ridges, leaving an orange band along the edge of the desert. We rode in circles, Justice and I. We tried one direction and then another as the easy heat of day slowly stiffened into a cool night breeze. I wished for a moon, not knowing whether it would be out that night or not.

The minutes stretched and pulled like taffy. Time plodded as slowly as Justice's disheartened walk. Nothing moved quickly now except the thoughts that banged around inside my head. I could not stop them, could not focus my mind on anything. *Gotta find Malcolm, gotta get back to camp, gotta let Justice rest, gotta keep going, gotta stop and find a place to sleep, gotta get out of this mess.* I started to cry.

Then I thought of Malcolm and what he said

about tending sheep alone out on Black Rock for weeks at a time. I was scared and I was alone, but I wasn't going to die. I reached deep inside me and hoisted up some hope, stopped sniveling, and began to hum my favorite songs.

It was dark now—thick, black dark. I stopped Justice for a moment. He let out a long, sad moan that tapered toward the end into a high-pitched sigh. After that there was solid silence. We stood in the silence for a long time, until it grew so dense and real around me that I couldn't bear it any longer. I kicked Justice hard and made him move on. And then I began to sing. Alone in the darkness, lost and drifting across the Joshua Slope, I began to sing a song my father used to sing when I was a kid.

"Well my daddy left home when I was three,
Didn't leave much to Ma and me,
Just this ol' guitar and an empty bottle of booze.
Now I don't blame him because he run and hid,
But the meanest thing that he ever did,
Was before he left, he went and named me Sue."

When I finally ventured a look at my watch, it was almost ten o'clock. Justice was lathered at the shoulders and blowing hard but I kept pushing him through the darkness. I saw nothing but the vague outline of Joshua trees as they passed in the night. My eyelids grew heavy and I struggled to hold them open. For one instant I fell asleep in the saddle and Justice brushed close to a Joshua. One of its spines pierced my shoulder, puncturing the skin like a poison dart. Suddenly I was wide awake. I grabbed my shoulder and clenched my teeth against the pain.

I pushed Justice deeper and deeper into the night until, finally, he stopped. One moment he was moving, the next he was stiff as a statue. I pressed my heels into his ribs and felt him freeze against me. It was as if he had walked into a brick wall. I swung out of the saddle, plunged onto legs of rubber, and tumbled to the ground. Justice stood firm in his place. I reached and grabbed a stirrup, then slowly pulled myself up. There was no feeling in my legs, only the prickly sensation of a million tiny needles. For a long time I leaned on Justice until my legs grew steady beneath me. I untied the cinch and pulled the saddle down, let it and the pads fall to the rocks at my feet, then unsnapped a bridle rein and wrapped the leather strap in a figure eight around Justice's two front hooves.

Fumbling in the darkness, I set and tied the makeshift hobbles the way Dad had taught me. I pulled the bridle over Justice's ears and let the bit drop out of his mouth. With his front legs bound together he hopped halfheartedly into the night. There would be no water, I was certain, but at least he could forage for grass without wandering too far before morning.

I set out the sweaty saddle pads for a bed and arranged the saddle as a headrest. I thought about my dad and the two other men back at the Upper Well—how they would be settling in for the night, crawling into warm bedrolls on comfortable cots. I wondered what Dad was thinking, whether he was worried in his heart or angry in his mind. Probably both, I thought. Probably angry, mostly.

I kept the driest saddle blanket to pull over my shoulders. There was nothing more to do than lie down. I was dead tired but knew that sleep would not come easily now, so I settled onto my hard bed and tried to think myself asleep.

I scanned the sky for the Big Dipper and couldn't find it anywhere. Then I remembered the cookies.

There were six of them. Three in each shirt pocket. I ate them all in a few quick gulps, not thinking about tomorrow.

When I swallowed the last cookie, I realized I was thirsty. I hadn't thought about water until now. The dry cookies had brought to mind a deep thirst that I had suppressed all afternoon. I recalled a canteen dangling from Malcolm's saddle and wondered why Dad hadn't sent one with me. Maybe he had forgotten. Or maybe that was one of those things he expected me to think of on my own. Either way, I had no water and I would have given the ten-dollar bill rolled up in my pocket for Malcolm's canteen, would have drunk from it in spite of Malcolm's disgusting lip protection technique. At that moment water seemed more precious to me than pride.

Lying on the pads with my head on the saddle, I stared into the night and soon became lost in the stars. I started to count them. There had to be millions of stars, and still it was the darkest night I had ever seen—no moon, just blackness broken by countless miniature specks.

Again I looked for the Big Dipper, but it was drowned in a sea of stars. Then I heard a high-pitched cry. It was quick and faint and I wasn't sure if it was the whine of a coyote or something else. I lay stiff and quiet for several seconds, my heart bouncing, waiting for another sound. It never came and I thought that maybe I'd been watching too many movies lately.

From where I lay I could see the outline of a Joshua tree against the night. I rubbed my shoulder where the Joshua spine had poked me. The pain came from deep in my arm. I thought of the tree that stabbed me, the Joshua that had grown in that same spot for a hundred years, maybe two, maybe three hundred years. It had stood there, I thought, the same tree in the same place, through the nights of a thousand seasons. It had been there when Abe Lincoln built his first split-rail fence. And it had been there when Babe Ruth hit his first home run. It had stood there through all the days and nights and years and ages—waiting for this lost, lonely night to stab me in the shoulder with one of its spines.

Time meant nothing to the tree, I thought. One night was no different from a thousand others. But to me, now, time was the enemy. I was ready to give everything I had for time to disappear, for the night to be over and for morning to be here. I considered the tree and how it waited, how it patiently accepted time's slow travel. If I could only be like the tree, I thought, I could close my eyes and open them and be sixteen.

I pulled the saddle blanket over my shoulders. It covered me only from the waist up. I longed for a radio and scolded myself for not borrowing Michael Bonner's Walkman. I imagined a set of saddlebags tied snugly to my saddle, full of candy bars and pop, and a radio.

There would be a Dodgers game tonight, I remembered. If only I could hear Vin Scully's voice. I'd feel better then, just like at night on my bed at home, that magical voice filtering through the feathers of my pillow. Vin Scully, the voice of baseball dreams.

The Dodgers would be playing at Candlestick. Will Clark would probably knock one out for the Giants. I'd hear the crack of the bat, the ring of wood on the ball, all the way out here on the Joshua Slope, clear out here in the middle of nowhere, where I was lost and alone in the universe—unless Hershiser was pitching. Clark wouldn't park one off Hershiser.

And then—I thought—and then the game would be over and I would dial in "All-Night Rock." I would listen to Rockin' Robby and hear the latest discs. I would listen until one or two o'clock in the morning—even three, if I wanted. Mom would not stick her head in the door and tell me to turn it off. I could listen to the radio all night.

The waves were right there—the radio waves. They were there in the thick night air, zapping through the sky at the speed of light. I couldn't catch them, though, couldn't tune into the waves without a radio.

7

I fell asleep and dreamed of crows.

Crows everywhere—sailing over the Joshua Slope, circling Signal Peak. They know where they have come from and where they are going and how to get back. They know because they are crows and crows take the shortest, straightest route and they can see the country. They don't need a map. The earth is their map. They see Salt Pond and the bald knoll and the Upper Well, see everything at once.

The crows are all headed to one place. They float

toward a dark speck in the desert, wing sharply to-ward a boy who lies spread-eagle on a lumpy bed of saddle blankets, his head propped up on a saddle.

The boy is asleep. He lies motionless on top of a ridge, next to a tall Joshua whose crooked arm reaches toward the mountain.

The sky is thick with crows. They swarm and land, float in from all directions and cover the ground around the sleeping boy. Or is he sleeping? It is mid-day and the sun pounds. A fly buzzes across the boy's face, lights on his nose, and crawls around his nos-trils. A crow hops onto the boy's stomach, dances on his chest, flutters its coal black wings, and groans a boastful caw. The boy does not move. He is not there. Only the shell of the boy is there.

Now the crow hops onto the boy's chin. Oily black, the crow perches proudly on the boy's chin. Ready now, the crow takes aim with its beak, zeroes in on the boy's eye with a pin-sharp beak.

Quick as a snake, the crow . . .

I awoke with a start and waved my arms across my face. I was smothered in darkness. The sky was as black as the crows in my dream. Then my eyes fixed on Justice, whose prickly chin was only a foot or so above my face. He stood there like a giant looking down at me, puzzled, licking his muzzle with his long tongue and reaching for the cookie crumbs still scattered across my shirt. I felt my chin and realized that just moments earlier the horse had licked it. My heart galloped, but I no longer felt alone. Justice needed company, too. We would stick this night out together.

When I awoke the next morning, I flipped over in a panic. Sunshine splashed across the Joshua Slope and flashed in my face. I squinted against the morning as my tender eyes fought off the light. The sun had lifted well above the eastern ridges but still had not burned off the morning cold. I felt a hollow chill all the way to my soul. It was the kind of chill that comes from more than being cold; it was the kind that comes from being both cold and lost.

My mouth was as dry as the rocks I had slept on. My legs ached in their new, bowed shape. When I sat up, my bones clattered as if they needed oil.

There stood Justice, his belly full of cheatgrass, his flanks gaunt for lack of water. He was waiting. He seemed ready to go, as if nothing was wrong and it was time to get back to whatever we were supposed to be doing. His eyes had hope in them and they seemed to say, "Let's go."

The thought of getting back was a good thought, but first things first. I was still lost. Besides that, a heavy weight in my chest reminded me that the most difficult part would be facing my father. It would be embarrassing for him, I knew. It would be hard for him to come to terms with a boy who could not make a simple swing around a bald knoll and meet a man back at Salt Pond in two hours.

I was thirsty, hungry, and cold. But mostly thirsty. At home there would be orange juice in the fridge, a tall half gallon of fresh juice in a plastic pitcher waiting cold on the top shelf. I would have drunk it all, would have gulped the entire two quarts in five seconds flat; but I was a long way from home.

I saddled Justice and untied his hobbles. He wheezed a dry cough and I realized that he must be as thirsty as I was. I gathered the reins and threw them over his neck and started to get on. Before I could poke my foot into the stirrup, Justice took off at a trot. I jerked back the reins. "Where do you think *you're* headed this morning?" I grumbled. Justice blew his nose on my sleeve and turned his head in the opposite direction from where I thought we should go. The revelation finally struck me—how stupid I had been. It came down like a two-by-four over my skull.

Justice was not lost.

I was the one who was lost.

Justice had never been lost. He knew that country as well as I knew my way to school. All I had to do now, and all I would have had to do yesterday, was simply drop the reins. Justice would have carried me straight to Salt Pond. He had wanted to all along— tried to—but I was too scared or stubborn or stupid to let him go.

Justice turned and looked at me again. It seemed a look of disgust, the kind of look that makes you glad animals can't talk.

On nothing but good old original horse sense, Justice could carry me back without a hitch. He could follow the map in his memory bank, or just let his nose guide him to the water at Salt Pond.

With an odd mix of pride at discovering the solution, and embarrassment at not realizing it sooner, I set Justice on automatic pilot and settled in for the ride.

8

◀◀◀○▶▶▶

Thirty minutes later we arrived at Salt Pond. Justice galloped up to the water's edge and waded in for a drink. I let him draw a long guzzle, then backed him out so he wouldn't stifle on too much water too fast. I slid off to get a drink myself, falling belly first to the ground and crawling up to the edge of the pond. Like a horse I sucked muddy water from the surface of Salt Pond, straining it through my teeth. I didn't care how it tasted.

Midgulp I heard a voice.

"What took you so long?"

I jumped to my feet. Malcolm sat on the bank above the pond. Witch stood with her reins dangling on the ground just a few steps away.

"Took me so long?" My lips quivered with surprise and fright.

"Thought you was gonna meet me back here in two hours."

"You *waited*?" I asked.

"A plan is a plan," replied Malcolm.

"You didn't really wait," I said. "You must have gone back to camp."

Malcolm grinned. He sat on the rock with his short legs pulled up to his chest and his greasy hat tipped back on his head. He looked like a scheming little leprechaun. With his chin in the air he took the last puff of a crumpled cigarette and flipped it into the pond. It seemed inconsiderate to me that he would throw his poisonous trash into the pond where Justice, I, and a good share of the cattle on the Joshua Slope might want to get a drink.

My heart rate slackened as the surprise of seeing Malcolm wore off. I studied him for some clue as to whether he had really waited, or if he was leading me on. His grin struck me as quite sinister and suggested some ancient ancestral trait for hating boys my age. Behind his dark eyes I sensed the gears of his mind churning, and thought that he must be happy with where he had me now, and was plotting his next nightmare for me.

"Where's your cattle?" he finally asked.

"I didn't see any."

"You've been ridin' since yesterday afternoon and got no cattle to show for it?"

"I was lost," I said. "If there were any cows out there, I didn't see them."

Malcolm had a small herd waiting just over the pond bank. I helped him push them toward camp. The day grew warmer as we rode and it wasn't long before the chill I'd felt that morning melted out of me and a trickle of sweat rolled down the back of my neck. Malcolm said nothing more all the way back— except what he said to the cows, which was mostly four-letter words strung together in ways I'd never heard before.

It was getting close to noon when Malcolm and I topped the ridge above the Upper Well. The sharp smell of rabbitbrush burned in my nose. We pushed two dozen head of cows and calves over the crest and down toward the corrals. I stopped for a moment before starting down, stunned by the scene before me. At the bottom of the ridge there must have been well over a hundred head of cows and their calves in the dusty corrals, all of them bellowing an off-key tune. The cattle were packed between the fences and fit together in colorful patterns like a jigsaw puzzle the size of half a football field.

In the space of twenty-four hours Malcolm and Will had gathered a big share of the herd, had, by some form of cowboy magic, made all those animals appear out of nothing. I was completely aware that they had worked this miracle without me. They had done it all while I wandered lost on the Joshua Slope.

It was a glorious sight, the kind that sends a gust through your heart and sweeps your spirit to the clouds. But as I kicked Justice and urged him down the steep trail into camp, my soaring spirit quickly fell back to earth and settled heavily in my chest.

The cattle had been gathered—no thanks to me. Now I dreaded how it would be to look my father in the eye.

9

◀◀◀○▶▶▶

Dad hobbled out to the gate and opened it as Malcolm and I brought the cows in. The canyon was thick with dust and the sound of bawling cattle. It was very hot now. There was no wind and the dust the cows kicked up hung close in the air and stuck to the sweat on my face and arms. Dad swung the gate shut behind the last cow and looked up at me without any emotion on his face. I wondered if he was even slightly happy that I had not died of exposure out there on the Slope, that my eyes had not been pecked out by crows.

I rode over to the horse corral and swung out of the saddle. My knees ached. I stood next to Justice for a long time and tried to stretch my bowed legs back into their normal shape. Justice tugged at the reins and pulled toward the water trough. Dad's voice hit me from behind like a punch in the back.

"I suppose he's thirsty," Dad said. "Think about your horse before you think about yourself."

I turned toward Dad and held back the tears that were trying to break loose. Dad had stopped a few feet away and stood there sullen as a sergeant with that ugly brace on his leg. I wanted to run up to him and hug him, wanted something good to happen between us. But this was nothing but business for Dad.

"They went looking for you, but it was too dark," he finally said. "They started looking again at daybreak. Did you get cold?"

"A little," I said. "I kept a saddle blanket over my shoulders."

Dad pushed the soiled hat back on his head. His sweat-lacquered face terrified me; it was dark with beard stubble and dust, but there was a clean white line above his brow where the hat usually covered—a band of startlingly white and delicate skin.

"You okay?" he asked.

"Yes," I said. "Hungry, though."

The men had gathered a good share of the herd that morning while looking for me. They did not go out all that afternoon. They stayed in camp and let the horses rest, and talked and planned while they studied the cows in the corral. What had been a quiet camp was now a constant chorus of whining cattle. It was as if the cows took shifts, one section bawling until their lungs gave out, then another section taking over. The continuous bellowing bothered me. I was nervous and shaken enough as it was. I didn't need the clamor of the cows on top of everything else.

I had thought that when I got back to camp everything would be all right again. Now everything was worse. I didn't know where I stood with Dad, or how the other men felt, or what to expect next. It was almost as if I weren't there, as if I were still lost and wandering aimlessly out on the Slope—a lone boy in the wilderness.

Will was the only one who even gave me credit for being alive. He was the one who pulled the ice chest out and spread all the fixings to build a sandwich across the camp table. He was the one who came back after I'd finished downing three or four thick cold-cut sandwiches and helped me put all the stuff away. Will was the one who patted me on the shoulder and told me I looked awfully tired and probably ought to go lie down for a while.

I fished my bedroll out of the pile of gear where we'd unloaded it the day before and carried it up to an empty cot under an old cottonwood tree. The bedroll flopped open on the cot and spilled over the edges. I pulled off my boots for the first time in two days and lay down on the covers. The last thing I remembered before gliding off to sleep was the voice of my father telling stories down by the fire.

10

◀◀◀○▶▶▶

I slept as stiffly as a tree, awaking only once in the cold night to crawl under the heavy covers of the bedroll. Time did not exist during those hours, did not even begin again until Dad shook my shoulder at five o'clock the next morning.

"Hop up," Dad said. "You've got a big one today."

It was cold and dark and I didn't know where I was. My mind would not kick in. It was locked in that border between sleep and awake, floating in a mystic middle space where everything seemed okay. Like a sluggish engine on a winter morning, I needed a jump-start.

Then I heard voices. It was Will and Malcolm a few yards away at the fire. They were discussing the day ahead. Will's voice was so soft I couldn't decipher what he was saying. Malcolm's words ground out like rocks through a crusher. It was the harsh sound of Malcolm's voice that kicked my mind over and started it running where it had left off the day before, turned it over to the truth and the discomfort of how things really were. Then Will spoke again and his voice settled over me like a warm blanket. Will's voice was soothing and sure and full of enough hope to charge me with the energy I needed to climb out of bed and pull on my boots and scurry down through the brush to the truck where my coat was tucked behind the seat.

Dad already had coals glowing beneath the Dutch oven. With the confidence of a chef he broke a dozen eggs and plopped them into the thick black cast-iron skillet, then tossed the shells into the fire. He cut open a package of sausage with his pocketknife and dumped the entire pile of links into the eggs. Suddenly the early morning air was full of the smell of breakfast.

"Mighty fine cook, you are," old Malcolm said. His mouth watered. By the firelight I could see the moistness between his earwaxed lips. Will sat quietly in his tattered lawn chair and Dad went on about his cooking in a businesslike way.

I pulled my plate out of the big metal dishpan and held it out to Dad. He spooned three large, steaming heaps onto it and I ate the sausage and scrambled eggs in large gulps. It was my first hot meal since arriving on the Slope. I topped it off with two slices of cold bread smothered in butter and strawberry jam.

After we cleaned up breakfast, Dad approached me. He was chewing on a twig of blackbrush, a makeshift toothpick. He nibbled on the twig and debated with himself for a long time before he spoke. I could tell when he finally came to his conclusion; it was when he pulled the stick from his mouth and flipped it to the ground. Then he looked me square in the eyes and said, "You'll be riding Buck today."

I turned away when he said it.

"Justice might like a day off," he said. "And Buck needs some use."

When Dad first said the word *Buck,* every muscle in my body tightened. I didn't even want to hear the horse's name, much less ride him. For an instant I tried to believe I had not heard anything. But the moments passed and Dad still looked straight at me with a flare in his eyes and I could not deny the echo in my mind—*You'll be riding Buck today.*

I'd never ridden Buck before. He was a green-broke, three-year-old colt and Dad had only been on the horse a few times himself. I was afraid of Buck; I had good reason to be. But I was even more afraid of admitting it to my father.

The memory of what happened on a winter afternoon just a few months earlier came flickering back through my mind. The scene passed before me as if I were sitting at a horror movie watching the screen. We were at the feedyard that cold afternoon. Dad was brushing the colt, speaking softly, trying to calm him. I walked up to them at the wrong time, not thinking, and suddenly raised my voice. The horse spooked, rearing back on the halter rope tied fast to the pipe panel fence. The chain reaction that began with a misspoken word quickly billowed into an explosion. Buck's front legs lifted off the ground and he pawed at the sky. As he reared back, the heavy fence came crashing down on Dad's knee. The knee bent backward, blew clean out of the socket, and Dad's leg collapsed the wrong way. I heard and felt his heavy moan of pain. My legs melted into rubber and my stomach turned at the sight of Dad's knee folded over. I was sick, terrified, helpless. There he lay, rolling and groaning. I turned away and started running on mushy legs, hightailed it all the way to Ben Walker's place a quarter mile down the road. Ben heard my panicked cries for help long before I got there. He met me in the driveway and we launched into his pickup and sprayed a rooster tail of dust all the way back to the feedyard. We loaded Dad in the back of the truck and sped into town to the hospital.

Buck did it.

No. *I* did it.

Buck pulled the fence over on Dad and it was my fault because I spooked the horse, couldn't keep my mouth shut when I should have known better. And then I left him, couldn't even help my dad because I was sickened at the sight and felt like throwing up and didn't know what to do. A few days later, when Dad came home from the hospital, he was different. He had grown bitter and cold. Ever since then he hadn't had much to say to me.

Now here we were on the Slope, the three of us together again: my father, Buck, and me—for the first time since that horrible winter afternoon.

"I don't want to ride Buck," I finally answered.

"You'll ride him," Dad said.

I felt like crying, but I didn't. I also felt like begging, but I couldn't. I wished that my father would just once put himself in my place and see things through my eyes. If he cared anything at all about me, he would not make me ride Buck.

But he did.

I sat next to the breakfast fire and didn't look up while Dad saddled Buck. I wasn't about to saddle him. If Dad wanted me to ride Buck, he could saddle the colt himself. It didn't matter to me if work like that was hard on Dad's leg. In fact, I hoped it made his leg roar with pain.

Time passed in a flash and Buck was ready too soon. "Come on," Dad called from the corral. "The day's not started until you're horseback."

Will took Buck's lead rope and snubbed the colt's nose up close to his saddle horn, taking two dallies around the horn and holding Buck frozen in his tracks so I could get on. Dad grabbed my left ankle as I lifted it and helped me reach my boot into the stirrup. My leg shivered like an electric toothbrush.

"You're not scared, are you?" Dad growled. He said it as if he would never have dreamed of being scared.

"Just cold," I said.

"You'll warm up soon enough," Dad said. He seemed relieved that I wasn't shaking out of fear.

The three of us—Malcolm, Will, and I—rode into the gray morning. The sun had just begun to bulge over the Slope and light spread slowly across the desert with its trailing hint of warmth. I sat as weightlessly and inconspicuously as I could atop Buck. When we crested the ridge above the Upper Well, I looked back and saw Dad down in camp, relaxed in a lawn chair, his crippled leg extended toward the fire.

Buck danced beneath me. His spirit seemed larger than his body that morning. He trotted and pranced as that unpredictable spirit swelled inside him, struggling to escape. It was a long time before I felt well enough in control to talk. Finally, after Buck settled a little, I asked Will where we were headed.

"Dodge Spring," he said. "About four miles out.

We're going after the freethinkers, the ones that go their own way. These won't be the rank and file animals. They'll have some personality, and they'll require some handling. Might get a little Western."

I smiled at Will as he talked. There was music in his voice and rhythm in his words. It felt good to be with Will.

The prospects for warmth increased as the sun rose, but the morning was still brisk—not too cold, but just enough to send a buzz through you. I was amazed at how cold it could get at night on the Slope, and how crisp the mornings were even though the days could heat up like an oven. The morning chill was not working in my favor; it seemed to keep Buck on his toes. Just when I thought he had settled down for good, he began to lift his feet high off the ground and started prancing like a parade horse.

I grew stiff in the saddle. It is easy to tell when a horse is on the edge of blowing, and I knew Buck was dancing on that edge.

Will rode close by. He kept an eye on Buck and me. Malcolm had moved out ahead of us and soon dropped over a ridge, disappearing into his own grumpy little world.

Will kept watching us as we hip-hopped through the blackbrush. "That there pony is a firecracker," he finally said.

"With an awful short fuse," I added.

"Just take him easy and you won't light it," Will said. "Another mile under his cinch and he'll settle in."

Will's words encouraged me. Riding next to him shored up my confidence. But deep inside I knew that if it came to a showdown, I was on my own. All the Wills in the world couldn't help me if Buck decided to come apart.

We rode further and further into the desert and before long I fell into a false sense of security. I sank into thoughts about home and school and what my buddies were up to just then. My mind floated away, leaving the business of Buck unattended. Suddenly, without any warning, a flop-eared jackrabbit blasted out of a bush beneath Buck. Someone might as well have thrown a grenade under the horse. All the spirit compressed inside Buck instantly burst. I felt the explosion, all four legs like rockets thrusting, the G forces between my legs. Then he came down with a crash and my groin smashed against the saddle as the horse quickly shot back up again. I gathered in the reins and jerked Buck's head around and he reared and spun and shot into the air again—up and down once more. My boots slipped out of the stirrups and I lost my bind in the saddle. I dropped the reins and grabbed the horn with both hands and vaguely heard Will hollering—something about not letting go of the reins. But it was too late now. It was over. Buck completely unhinged beneath me and I launched into a free fall. For one extended moment I floated in the morning air before I came down in a slapping heap at the foot of a Joshua tree.

Everything faded—my vision, my thoughts, the pain. Then the world began to focus around me and my mind became suddenly crisp and the pain screamed through me.

Will was there in a heartbeat. He held my head up, asked me where it hurt, told me not to move.

"I'm okay," I said. "I think I'm okay."

"Don't move," Will said.

In the meantime, Buck kicked and snorted and ran back toward camp. I could hear the trailing sound of his hooves as he crossed the next ridge over. I was horseless now. That was all I could think of. Horseless and hopeless. I needed to cry, but Will was squatting right there next to me, looking down at me like a doctor. I couldn't cry in front of Will.

71

But I did.

The tears gushed out as if from behind a broken dam. I couldn't stop them. I hurt all over—inside and outside, all the way through. Amid the pain I remembered Dad sprawled on the cold ground last winter, his leg bent and him lying alone after I had turned away. Then I looked up at Will's weathered face hovering above me. He had taken off his dark glasses and I could see deep into the blue pools of his eyes. He was there and I needed somebody to be there.

I rolled over and tried to hide my crying. I'd have to walk back now. I'd have to face Dad and somehow try to justify my being here on the Joshua Slope, explain why I was here if all I could do was get lost and get thrown and cause everyone to spend more time looking for me and worrying about me than gathering cows like we were supposed to be doing.

Finally the pain began to fade and I stopped my sniveling. By now Will was convinced that my back was okay. He helped me sit up, brushed the dust and the gravel off my pants, and set my hat on my head.

We both noticed my arm at the same time. The skin on my left arm, from the wrist to the elbow, was ground up like hamburger and embedded with small chunks of rock.

"We best get you back to camp and clean you up," Will said. "Come on, I'll ride you in."

"I can walk," I said. "You go ahead with Malcolm. I'll walk back to camp."

"I'll ride you back," Will said. "Ol' Roddy rides good double. Malcolm's fine. He's long gone anyway."

11

◀◀◀○▶▶▶

Will climbed on his horse, then reached down and pulled me up behind him. We headed back through the brush toward camp, where Buck had probably already arrived, alerting Dad to the fact that something was wrong. Sure enough, something was wrong again and his son had messed up again, and Dad would wonder why he even bothered to bring me along, why he didn't just leave me home and make do as best he could in spite of his mangled knee.

Will's horse moved smoothly through the tangled brush. I held on to the cantle of Will's saddle with the hand of my good arm and let the injured arm dangle free at my side. It felt like it had been worked over with a sledgehammer. I kept my mind off it by concentrating on Will's whistling. He whistled constantly as he rode, mostly tunes I'd never heard before.

I wanted to start a conversation, so I asked him why he called his horse Roddy.

"That's his nickname," Will answered. He continued his whistling. A moment later he added, "His registered name is Hot Rod Hank. But I like to call him Roddy."

We rode on for a while and Will kept whistling.

"What's that song?" I asked as we passed dangerously close to a Joshua tree.

"You don't know that one?" Will asked in dismay.

"Never heard it before."

"That's one of the all-time greats," Will replied. He began to sing the words: "Hello my baby, hello my honey, hello my ragtime gal."

"Catchy tune," I said.

"Of course it is," Will said. "You young folks nowadays got no use for the great songs. All you wanna hear is that yeah-yeah-yeah stuff. Shoot, you can't even understand the words." Now Will was starting to sound like Malcolm, but I had discovered a difference between the two: I knew I could reason with Will. He would hear me out. Malcolm, all he would do is put up a stone wall.

"How about this," I said. I started to sing a tune I thought he'd like, a song from one of my Rod Stewart CDs called "Forever Young." It was a slow song with a beautiful melody and the kind of good lyrics an old man could understand.

"I like that," Will said. "That ain't one of those yeah-yeah-yeah songs."

"It's Rod Stewart," I said. "You ever heard of Rod Stewart?"

"Oh, certainly," Will said. "He used to run cows down on the Tuly Desert. Funny thing, I never knew he had musical inclinations." Will flicked the reins over Roddy's neck and the horse picked up the pace.

I explained to Will that we must be talking about two different Rod Stewarts, since mine was a rock star from England who had probably never been anywhere near the Tuly Desert. Will shrugged his shoulders and said, "Ain't that something."

My arm was on fire, but bantering with Will kept the pain at a distance, and kept my mind off Dad.

For the second day in a row I dreaded how it would be when I got back to camp.

Will turned around in the saddle and looked at me. "How old were you when your Grandpa Winsor died?" he asked.

"I was just a little kid," I said. "I can't really remember him. There's a picture in a scrapbook at home that shows me sitting on a horse with him. I was just a baby."

"Too bad," Will said. "It's too bad you never got to know him. He was a fine, fine man. I rode a million miles with Isaac Winsor."

"Wish he was still here," I said. "I'd give anything to talk to him and ride with him and hear his stories."

"Your father's cut from the same cloth," Will said.

I didn't say anything.

We passed a clump of bushes with large green leaves and beautiful trumpetlike flowers. The flowers were bigger than my fist and white as the billowing morning clouds. There was just one clump of plants and they looked as out of place here as a McDonald's would have looked. "What *are* those things?" I asked Will.

"Moonlily," he said. "Pretty, aren't they?"

"Yeah," I said. "I've never seen flowers so white."

"Don't let 'em fool you," Will said. "That there moonlily is worse than arsenic. If a cow ate one mouthful of those leaves, she'd be history. Indians used to use it for medicinal purposes, but very, very carefully. It's dangerous stuff."

"It's about the prettiest thing I've seen out here," I said.

"Things aren't always what they seem," Will said.

As we drew closer to camp, Will turned once more in the saddle and looked at me point-blank. "That's a funny-lookin' haircut you got there," he said. I felt like I was with Malcolm again. Will must have gotten a good look at my hatless head after Buck threw me.

I was lost for words. My razor cut looked just like all the other guys' at school. I didn't see anything funny about it.

"That's one thing I can't figure about your generation," Will said. "Why you'd want to cut your hair so silly. Women, I can understand them messing with their hair all the time. But why would a man want to fuss when a good standard cut will do?"

It bothered me that Will didn't care for my haircut. I wanted him to like it, wanted him to like *me*. Yet somehow I didn't feel he was accusing me of anything. He just seemed curious; that was all. Even so, I felt a powerful need to justify to Will the way I looked.

"Everybody at school wears their hair this way," I said.

Will turned and smiled. "I see," he said. "And suppose everybody started eatin' cow pies for breakfast?"

I searched deep inside my razor-cut head for a reply and came up with nothing. The case was closed.

Soon we reached the ridge above camp. Will stopped Roddy and we gazed down at the scene. Dad sat in his lawn chair next to the fire, his leg propped up on a log. Buck, still saddled, was tied to the fence, pawing up a storm in the dirt. Will nudged Roddy with the heels of his boots and we started down the trail into camp.

My heart sank a little lower with each step.

12

◀◀◀○▶▶▶

Dad hoisted himself slowly from his chair as we rode up. His face was solemn and he stood in the warm breeze like an old tree. More than anything I wanted him to ask if I was all right, but all he said was, "What happened?"

Will related how the rabbit broke beneath Buck and how Buck still had an edge on him and how the horse came off the ground as if a land mine had exploded beneath him—about as high as he'd ever seen a horse pitch, and how I landed on my arm next to a Joshua tree and how I needed to wash it up, and then we could get going again.

Dad heard Will out, but didn't respond. He stood there thinking a minute, then turned and hobbled toward the fire. He pulled a kettle off the coals and poured some hot water in a round washbasin on the camp table. I slid off Roddy's rump and landed on aching feet. Dad motioned me toward the fire. I walked slowly and felt the pain shoot through me; the aftershocks of my crash. Dad handed me a bar of soap and I washed my arm as best I could, delicately picking out each tiny chunk of rock. When I finished, he handed me a towel. I tried to look my father in the eyes but my pride was hurt worse than my arm, and as soon as our eyes made contact they kicked off in other directions like colliding marbles. I wanted to tell Dad how the horse spooked, how he panicked just like he had the day he was tied to the pipe panel fence, how he had a wild streak in him and maybe he wasn't our kind of horse, and maybe we ought to get rid of him.

But Dad didn't want to talk about what had *already* happened. He was more interested in what was *going* to happen now. "Are you ready to get back on?" he asked.

"If you say so," I said. "My arm hurts."

"It'll hurt whether you ride or not."

"I'd rather ride Justice," I said.

"Justice has the day off," Dad said. "Buck needs the use. Get on him and gallop him a stretch—I should have had you do that in the first place. It'll take the edge off him. He'll be fine once you knock the edge off him."

"I'd honestly rather ride Justice," I said, trying desperately to hold back the tears.

Dad's eyes brimmed with disgust. He looked down at the ground and lamely kicked a rock with his braced-up leg. The contraption on his knee seemed to weigh a thousand pounds.

"I brought you out here to help me," Dad growled. "I brought you out here to be an asset, not a liability. I need you to gather cows, and I need you to ride Buck. There's a job to be done here and that's the only thing that matters right now."

13

I got back on Buck and galloped him down the wash, ran him hard through the sandy bottoms. I kicked him and pushed him until sweat broke from his shoulders and his neck began to lather. I whipped the reins across his rump and imagined that he was my father, drove him harder than he wanted to go. I forced him to run until I could feel his heart boom between my legs, until the giant pounding spirit inside him shrank to a manageable size and he was mine.

Then I rode back up the trail with Will.

We rode all the way to Dodge Spring and flushed

out fifty head of cows and almost as many calves along the way. We rooted them out of the draws, the hollows, and the thick brush. They were wilder cattle than the others we had gathered. They ran out ahead of us and many of them kept trying to break away from the herd. I was nervous and on my toes, wanting to do everything right for Will. At Dodge Spring we let the cattle settle around the water hole while our horses drank. Buck was dead tired. The spirit possessing him that morning had disappeared like a puff of smoke.

Halfway back to camp we met Malcolm with a sizable herd of his own. The cattle were weary and subdued by now. The afternoon sun beat down on us like a heat lamp and slowed everything to a crawl. We brought all the cattle in together, herded the rolling fat cows and their tired little calves moaning and bawling and sore-footed into camp. I followed the last of the cows through the gate, rode whooping and hollering behind them, and pushed them through the narrow opening with authority. Dad closed the gate and looked at me as if maybe I was becoming more of an asset than a liability. But he didn't say anything like that to me after I unsaddled and took care of Buck and came to the fire for supper.

Dusk settled like a shroud over the canyon. Potatoes and hamburger steaks simmered in the Dutch oven. The smoky smell of food in the evening air made my stomach grind. I set my hat on a bush, squatted near the fire, and ate my share of supper like a wolf over a lamb.

For a long time after I finished eating I sat on a stump near the fire waiting for some kind of encouragement. Dad said nothing about Buck or about how I had done. He had other things on his mind. Apparently my feelings weren't a priority at the moment. Nothing seemed to matter to him now but the cows and the long push that lay ahead.

Later I got up and wandered out into the brush. I found a long, flat rock that looked like a park bench and sat down alone. The world grew darker by the minute. I spent the rest of the evening there, just within earshot of three voices that rose and floated across the night air like smoke from the fire. There was still a sting in my arm, but it was insignificant compared to the burning in my chest— the desire that flared inside me to make my father proud of me, to find my place in this outfit, to feel comfortable and welcome and a part of the circle.

14

Dad and the others told stories late into the night.

The cattle were mostly gathered and the drive would begin in the morning. It was time for some serious storytelling now, time to recount tales of long-ago days on the Joshua Slope. My father loosened up for the stories, became happy and bright and animated. I sat alone on my rock bench in the darkness and listened as he talked of his great-grandfather Ammon Winsor, who had settled on Clover Mountain in the 1860s. He retold the story to Malcolm and Will about how Ammon Winsor had befriended the

Indians, the Paiutes from down on the Muddy River. Great-Grandpa Winsor had gained their respect with a simple mix of honesty and kindness.

Under the stars and next to the crackling fire Dad told more stories. I had heard some of them before, but many of them were new to me. I thought of each story as a piece of a giant puzzle, and imagined that if I could hear them all and put them together where they fit, the finished puzzle would look like the Slope itself.

One of the stories caused Dad to slow down and talk in respectful tones. It was one about Josh Whitaker. Old Josh had lived nearly all his life on the Slope. "Toughest old piece of leather that ever lived," Dad exclaimed.

From my seat out in the brush I could see Will and Malcolm nodding their heads in reverence. "Josh Whitaker," Dad repeated, shaking his head as if he still could not believe what he was about to relate. "He was no more than twelve years old when he brought that herd down the Slope. Alone. It was late in the fall and his father was laid up with pneumonia and they still had twenty or thirty head on the mountain when the snow hit. There was nobody but Josh to move those cows off the mountain and the boy rose to the occasion. He rode an old white horse named Traveler that knew the country inside and out. Took him three days to push those cattle out of the snow and move 'em down here to the Slope—nothing but a bedroll and a gunny sack with some canned beans and peaches and a carton of Mother's Oats tied to the back of the saddle."

Malcolm had been nodding his head and puffing on a cigarette through the first part of the story. He was anxious to take over now. "When I was a kid, I rode halfway around the world with Josh Whitaker," Malcolm said. "Seemed like he was an old man even then. Had a crooked arm, Josh did. And I'll tell you how he got it. It was on that same winter drive you was telling about, Jake. Somewhere comin' down off the mountain ol' Traveler stumbled in the snow and dumped Josh in the rocks. Broke the boy's arm. When he got back to town a few days later, his arm was swollen tight as a boxing glove. He had the arm tied in a splint made out of that Mother's Oats carton."

I knew Josh Whitaker. I had never seen him on a horse, but I knew what he looked like. Dad visited him every Christmas at the rest home, and one year he took me along. All I remembered was the wrinkled shell of a man slumped in a wheelchair, a sad-looking old fellow with thin gray hair who could barely lift his head, and how he answered my dad's questions in a weary, worn-out voice. Now I tried to think of Josh as a twelve-year-old boy, whooping and hollering and driving thirty head off the mountain through the snow and the cold. A brave and capable boy. The story made Josh alive and strong, and I ached inside to measure up to him.

I wanted to go to the fire and take my seat in the circle, but I didn't feel worthy. In fact, I wondered if I should even be listening. Dad was propped back in his lawn chair on the other side of the fire and I could see the wavering form of his face through the orange flames. The stories seemed like a reward the men were giving themselves for getting the cattle gathered. I had contributed very little to the job, and felt that I didn't deserve to hear. And yet I listened. Maybe hearing the stories would somehow help me become worthy of them. It was late and I was tired and my mind was circling back on me. I wondered how it would feel to be in the stories—not just to hear them and deserve them, but to actually be a part of them just like Will and Malcolm and my dad.

*   *   *

The men continued to talk as the night grew black and the easy evening air slowly turned cold. The stories flowed like a river and flooded my mind until I was full of them and nearly overcome by a chill that left me shivering. The talking went on long after I got up and stumbled through the rocks to my cot. I crawled into the cool blankets and tried to forget that my arm was on fire.

For a long time I lay beneath the heavy covers and looked up at the black sky and its countless stars. The air was still and I could hear the crackle of the fire and the muffled words and chuckles of the men. I turned my head slightly and there, startlingly clear, glowed the Big Dipper. It had been there all the time, as big as life. I followed the trail of the Dipper to its outer edge, then traced an imaginary line to the North Star, just as my father had taught me when I was a little boy. It was always in the same place—the North Star—the star that stood still. Lying warm in my bedroll, I recalled one of the Paiute legends I had included in my research paper for Mr. Mulligan's class.

It was the story of Nagah, the mountain sheep, who was a son of Shinob, the younger Paiute god. Nagah found a peak that reached as high as the clouds and he wanted to climb to the top of it to make his father proud. But the peak was too steep and too rough to climb. Nagah tried anyway; he didn't want to disgrace his father. He searched at length for a trail and finally found a cave. Entering into the darkness, he began to climb. The cave was full of loose rocks and a fearsome noise rose up through the darkness as rocks rolled and dashed to pieces below. Nagah struggled upward until his courage failed. He was afraid. He turned back and discovered that the rolling rocks had closed the cave below him. He had no choice now but to push on.

After a long time Nagah looked up and saw a speck of light. He pushed toward the light and soon emerged, finding himself on top of the peak. When Shinob saw his son standing so high in the sky, he was proud, so proud he turned Nagah into Pootsee, a star, and left him there to shine for everyone to see. Nagah became the only star that is always found in the same place.

I went to sleep with the stories and dreamed them. Only in my dreams did I become part of them.

15

I awoke to clouds. The morning of the drive was gray with thin, wispy clouds. I threw off the covers and tried to sit up, but my chest felt as if it were tied to the cot. I tried again and couldn't move. Finally I rolled out and onto my knees and from there hoisted myself up to standing position. The muscles in my back and arms and legs felt stiff as beef jerky. Slowly I worked each muscle until I finally moved freely enough in the chilly morning to pull on my pants and shirt.

Today we would begin the northward push. Nearly 300 head of cows and 250 calves stood ready down in the corrals. They were almost all the cattle on the Joshua Slope, as many as we expected to get. We would take what we had now and push them north across the Slope to Clover Mountain, up to the meadows where a cow could spend the summer getting fat.

After breakfast I walked a quarter mile down the dry wash to work out more of my stiffness. I was gone longer than I should have been, and when I got back Dad had already saddled Justice. My father's eyes flashed with his Where-have-you-been look. I quickly jumped on and rode over next to Will and Malcolm, who were both mounted on their horses and looked like they'd been waiting awhile. Dad hobbled off to the main corral and swung the gate wide. The cattle spilled out like water from a toppled pitcher. They flowed through the narrow funnel of the gate and spread out in a dusty haze. Will and Malcolm shot out on the wings, Will to the right and Malcolm to the left.

I slipped into the center on Justice, took my position behind the herd, and began to holler and whistle. Immediately, the hardier cattle trotted to the lead and settled into their places along the soft-shoulder edge of the road. Most of the animals remained in a tight group the width of the road and fifty yards deep. Among the slower cattle were several cows with brand-new little calves born within the last couple of weeks, and a handful of rotund others that waddled heavily and looked like they were ready to give birth any day now. Also at the rear of the herd were a half dozen rolling, fat bulls—the herd sires— all of them red except for one black Angus that I had been told belonged to Malcolm. For the most part, except for a few shortcuts, the cattle would stay on the rough excuse of a road and follow it twenty miles up the Joshua Slope until it reached the top of Clover Mountain.

My chest heaved with glory as the cattle trudged up the road. I felt a stirring sense of power trotting along behind, pushing the fat ones and cursing the lazy ones—yipping and yelling and whistling. I felt magnificently alive and aware. It was the same kind of buzzed and flurried feeling I got when rock music blared from the speakers of my stereo at home. It was a feeling my friends back at school would have a hard time relating to, and I wondered how I was going to explain it to them when all this was over and I was back in the neighborhood living a normal life. I realized then that most of this was something I would keep for myself.

Dad remained at the Upper Well for a couple of

hours. He planned to break camp and catch up with us in the truck about lunchtime. Will and Malcolm left their trucks parked at the Upper Well. Dad would shuttle them back down to get the trucks when the cattle drive was over.

We pushed the animals through the morning mist at a limber clip. The clouds slowly gathered and thickened above us. The cattle seemed invigorated by the cool, moist air. I rode at full attention behind them, swinging out now and then to pull in a cow or calf that strayed from the herd. One calf in particular wanted to make her own trail apart from the rest. She was a tiny, rust red calf, maybe a month old. She craned her tail high in the air and pranced gingerly alongside her mother near the back of the herd. Every few minutes the calf shot out through the blackbrush like a willowy deer, then returned in a flat-out charge to the herd. Each time she ventured a little farther out, as if testing me.

Will and Malcolm rode through the trees about fifty feet to either side of me. I saw them every few minutes—Will's palomino and Malcolm's gray, and the colors of their clothes flashing between the trees. Each time the little red calf ran off, Will and Roddy patiently brought her back to the herd.

95

"They've all got personalities," Will said as he brought the calf back to the herd for the third time. "They're just like people. Some take life seriously, and some just want to play."

I smiled and watched how most of the cows marched up the road with their heads down, all businesslike, while a few of them kept their noses in the air and seemed preoccupied with everything going on around them. Then I looked over at Will and watched him weave through the Joshuas. I admired how he rode the yellow gelding. He and Roddy seemed to move as one. Will looked noble atop his golden horse, in spite of the fact that his hat was old and soiled with an oily brown sweat line where the dust clung to it halfway up the crown. I knew I was watching a true horseman, and it occurred to me that if Will had been born in some other world where horses did not exist, he would have probably spent his life in search of such an animal.

The next time Will brought the little red calf back to the herd he stayed and rode alongside me for a while. He untied his rope from the saddle straps and began to swing it behind a plodding cow. I watched him twirl the rope in a smooth, level pattern. He swung the rope with style, the way the rodeo ropers did on the Fourth of July at Gunlock. On the last swing he dipped the loop over his left shoulder and dropped it perfectly in front of the cow's hind legs and, as the legs stepped into the loop, pulled it up tight on two hooves. Will could rope; that was certain. He could slip it on a cow's hind hocks with the same effortless skill as Eric Davis catching a fly ball in left field. Second nature. Routine.

"Here's how you learn to rope," Will said as we ambled along behind the herd. "Practice. Hours of practice. When you've roped that cow a thousand times, then you'll just be getting started. When you've roped her another thousand, you'll still be a beginner."

Will reached the rope across the space between Roddy and Justice and nodded for me to take it. I grabbed it, built a loop, and began swinging.

My arm ached and my shoulder was so stiff I could hardly raise the loop above my hat.

"It's all in the wrist," Will said.

I threw an awkward loop. It landed lamely in the dirt, nowhere near the target. The misguided rope spooked the little red calf and she darted off again, shot out through the brush like a miniature missile. Roddy almost moved before the calf did. He seemed to pick it all up on radar before it even happened. The horse pivoted in a flash to the right and Will didn't even shift in the saddle. They cut off the calf before she made daylight from the herd.

"He's an awfully nice horse," I said to Will as he rode back to my side.

"Roddy ranks with the best of 'em," Will said. His voice was still gruff, but soft. Roddy walked on in a smooth, quick gait. Will reined him with only a subtle flick of the fingers.

"I sure wish Justice could walk like your Roddy," I said.

"Now there's the thing about horses," Will replied. "You never get one that does it all. They're no different than people. You get one that turns on a dime, but then he don't know a cow from a coyote. Or you get one that works cows like a dream, such as these two here, and maybe he doesn't keep worth a dang. Take ol' Justice there," Will went on. "So he *can't* walk. Well, I bet he could outrun most every horse in the county. He's a fine all-around pony—good as you're gonna find. And then you take Roddy here. He walks out at a clipping pace and he handles cattle as nicely as you'd ever expect a horse to. But he don't have near the speed your horse does.

Ol' Justice there, he'd leave Roddy in the dust."

"Right now, I'd sooner Justice could walk than run," I said.

Will chuckled. His chin bobbed up and down with the rhythm of Roddy's quick walk.

Just then the little red calf shot out from the herd again. This time she got the jump on Roddy, whose eye was on another calf playing games along the far side of the herd. Will nudged Roddy's neck with the toe of his left boot and the horse spun to the right. Roddy took off so fast, exploded with such a burst, he left one of his hind shoes on the road.

The calf scampered into the trees and disappeared. Will and Roddy swung wide in pursuit. I stopped Justice and jumped out of the saddle. The freshly fallen horseshoe lay in the road, partially covered with dirt. I picked it up, dusted it off, and held it in my palm. It felt warm and alive, as if it were still part of Roddy's hoof. All of this was strangely magical, almost as if I were holding a living part of Roddy in my hand.

Will and Roddy finally returned with the rebellious calf. "That little gal reminds me of my kids when they were younger," Will said as he settled in next to me.

"How's that?" I asked.

"Always wantin' to take off on their own, runnin' out half-cocked with nary an idea where the hell they're goin'."

I chuckled. Then I showed the horseshoe to Will. "Roddy lost this," I said. "It came off when you took after the calf."

Will smiled until I saw all the gold in his teeth. "I've seen horses turn in their tracks before," Will said. "But I never saw one turn clean out of his shoe." He reached down and patted Roddy on the shoulder. I realized then that even though it meant extra work for Will to put the shoe back on, he was actually pleased that Roddy had turned hard enough to leave that little arc of iron in the road. I reached the horse-shoe toward Will. He shook his head, rejecting my offer. "Got a new one in the truck," he said. "I'll put it on him as soon as your dad catches up with us in the truck. Meantime, you'll have to take the right wing," he said. "I'll keep Roddy here on the soft shoulder."

Will probably expected me to throw the old shoe off to the side of the road. Instead, I tied the worn piece of iron to my saddle. I would keep it there until we got to camp—not realizing then that I would probably keep it the rest of my life.

16

◀◀◀○▶▶▶

I scooted Justice out to the right side of the herd, staying close enough so I could still visit with Will. He stopped once, got off Roddy, and inspected the hind hoof that had thrown the shoe. I saw him smile and shake his head and I could tell he was tickled with Roddy and the idea that he had turned hard enough to leave his shoe behind. After that, rather than get back on, Will stayed on his feet and walked for a while, leading Roddy, who ambled leisurely behind. I wasn't sure if he did it to give Roddy a break, or just to stretch his own tired old legs. Probably both, I thought.

We drove the cattle on, hooted and hollered and yipped them up the Joshua Slope.

After a long stretch Will got back on Roddy and we started visiting with each other as the cattle slowly pulled northward. Will asked me if I had a girlfriend.

I shook my head no. But my thoughts turned immediately to Christy Harris. She was an eighth grader and one of the finest girls at school. She and a couple of her friends had come over and talked to Michael Bonner and me during the Valentine's dance. I almost asked her to dance that night. And I was for sure going to ask her at the School's Out dance at the end of the year. But that was before the possibility evaporated when I agreed to help Dad on the Joshua Slope.

Christy Harris.

Sure, I had a girlfriend. It was just that *she* didn't know it.

Will didn't need to know it, either. That's why I shook my head no.

Riding along behind the herd, Will pointed out each of the brands on the cows: his own *Rocking-B* on the left shoulder, Malcolm's *M-Bar-H* on the left ribs, and, of course, my father's *Flying-W* on the right ribs, which I already knew. I studied the cows as they pulled up the road and read the brand on each one.

"How many children do you have?" I asked him.

"Four married daughters and a son," Will said. He smiled and thought for a moment, then added, "I waited a long time for that boy. All my girls came out here and helped me when they were younger—made mighty good hands while they lasted—but once they reached a certain age, other interests took over—namely boys—and they left me high and dry. The boy, though, he took to the Slope like a bird to the sky and he stayed with it until he joined the service."

"How old was he when he first came out here?" I asked.

"About your age."

"How old is he now?"

"He's twenty-five. He's a helicopter pilot down on the border," Will said. "He works for an aviation company in Tucson—hires out for the border patrol, and county sheriffs call him when somebody's lost. He patrols for illegal aliens, intercepts drug traffic, does a lot of search and rescue—that sort of business."

"What's his name?" I asked.

"William, Junior," Will said. "We call him Billy."

* * *

I bobbed along in my position at the right side of the herd and thought about Billy Buchanan down on the border. Mexico seemed light-years from the Joshua Slope, yet it was only one state away, and probably didn't look much different from the country we were crossing. If you rode there from here on your horse, staying clear of the towns and highways, you'd never even know when you crossed the line. You'd just ride until one day you were there. I thought of Billy in his helicopter on the border, looking for people who crossed a line you couldn't even see.

In the midst of my daydreaming the little red calf took another detour.

"Better bring 'er back," Will called from the road.

I came to my senses and reeled my mind all the way back from Mexico to the Joshua Slope. The calf had a good jump on me. I jabbed Justice in the ribs and he broke into a hard gallop. Hopping the blackbrush, we made a beeline for the calf.

"Swing wide!" Will yelled in his rough voice. "Swing wide!"

But it was too late to swing wide. Justice and I had already rushed in behind the calf and jammed her, startled her into running headlong away from the herd. We had flushed her into a terrible panic, the kind that fries a little calf's brain and causes her to flee with no thought of where she is or where she's going. Justice and I did exactly what we were *not* supposed to do. We took a simple situation and complicated it. My father had told me many times how to work young calves, how to approach them calmly and give them space—two or three times as much space as you'd give a grown cow. I had forgotten it all in my effort to impress Will. I had become a liability again.

The calf ran as if possessed, and my heart sank as she flew over the next ridge. Moments later Justice and I topped the same ridge. I pulled the horse to a stop and surveyed the next little valley. There was no calf in sight.

I heard Will calling from the road. "Come on back," he yelled. "Don't worry about her."

Don't worry about her?

I rode down the other side of the ridge, pushed Justice off the rocky slope for one more look. The calf could not have vanished. She had to be down in the draw somewhere. It was midday now and the clouds were breaking. A shaft of sun funneled through a hole in the sky and shone down on the landscape like a spotlight. No calf. No calf anywhere. She was gone. That was all.

The next ridge was a quarter mile off. I could not ride to it and look over into the next draw without falling far behind the herd. I turned Justice and galloped back toward the road, kicked him hard is if all this were his fault, and rode quickly and dejectedly back to Will.

"I must have scared her off," I said as I rode up next to Will and Roddy. "I can't see her anywhere."

I expected Will to be angry, but he just grinned. He grinned so hard the top of his dark glasses rose midway up his forehead.

It frustrated me. Sweat dripped from my brows. I took off my hat and rubbed my good arm across my face.

For fifty yards Will grinned. He didn't say anything, just rode along with his glasses pushed up above his eyebrows. I started to boil inside. I figured he was making fun of me because I was a green kid with a funny haircut, an awfully easy target. I was just about to let him know how I felt about him taking advantage of me like that. Then he spoke.

"See that bolly-faced cow up there on the right?" Will said.

"Sure," I indignantly replied. "I see her."

"That red devil of a calf you chased off belongs to her," Will said. "Now watch her. Any minute now she'll discover the calf is gone. It'll dawn on her just like that. She'll cut away from the herd and start looking for that delinquent little child of hers. When she does, just let her go. She'll find the calf a whole bunch easier than we will."

"So what do we do?" I asked. "Do we have to wait?"

"No sir," Will said, shaking his head. "That's an old cow, a veteran of the Slope. She knows the territory. She'll find her little wayward child and they'll make their own way to the mountain. No need to lose any sleep over it."

I looked at Will as he bobbed along on Roddy. It was hard for me to just let the cow and calf go, especially after we'd worked so hard to gather them and bring them this far. I believed Will, though—trusted every word he said. Will had a way of seeing the big picture. He knew the beginning and the middle and the end of things.

"They come back, Brian," he said. "You can chase 'em halfway to town and they'll always come back."

"You won't tell Dad, will you?" I pleaded. "Please don't tell him."

"Okay," Will said. "It's our story."

17

◀◀◀○▶▶▶

We rode on together, Will and I.

Up through the trees I caught a glimpse of Malcolm on his old gray mare.

"Why does Malcolm call his horse Witch?" I asked Will.

"Don't rightly know," Will said. "Maybe because she looks like one."

"But she's a fine-looking mare," I said.

"She *would* be if you put a gunnysack over her head," Will mused. "I'd say that head of hers is about two sizes big. That Roman nose don't flatter her much, neither."

I started to laugh. Sometimes the way Will said things made me laugh. I had gained plenty of confidence with Will by now, enough to ride shoulder to shoulder with him and laugh at things he said.

A little farther down the road I asked, "How come Malcolm's so grumpy?"

"That's just his way," Will answered.

"He seems to have something against me."

"Don't judge him too quickly," Will said. "You don't know Malcolm yet."

I thought about that for a while and watched Malcolm far off in the trees. I could hear him hollering at the cows in a hard, hateful voice. "Was he always like this?" I asked Will.

"Not when his kids were younger and he had some help on the place," Will explained. "He had a couple of boys who used to ride the Slope. They were pretty good hands, but they grew up and went to college and never came back. One of them is a highly respected plant man—botanist, they call him. Those boys of Malcolm's got lured into the modern world, and ol' Malcolm has little use for the modern world. I think he was born about a hundred years late."

"That doesn't explain why he's so grouchy," I said.

"There could be a lot of reasons for that," Will said. "His father abandoned the family when Malcolm was just a little shaver. Left without a trace. But the hardest thing for ol' Malcolm was when his wife passed on. She died of cancer about five years ago. He worshiped that woman, loved her more than life itself. I know he misses her. I know it 'cause I haven't seen him smile but a time or two since she died."

"Oh," I said. We rode along in silence for a while and I thought how there was always more to the story than you knew.

Pushing further up the Slope, I noticed the country slowly changing. The higher we climbed, the fewer Joshua trees there were. The Joshuas were replaced by more and more dark green juniper trees. Will and Roddy stayed behind the herd on the road. Justice and I kept watch on the right wing. Malcolm stayed to himself out in the trees on the left wing. Again, when the cattle had lined out nicely, I slipped in and rode next to Will. He handed me the rope and nodded for me to practice some more. I swung the loop and threw it at a cow, missing by a mile. Will gave me encouragement and more instructions, and I tried again.

I asked Will questions about his son, about how Billy had liked it out on the Slope, and what kind of hand he was.

Will's face glowed when he spoke of Billy. "It's not just anybody can fly those choppers," he said. "Takes a special kind of person. Not all brains, either. No sir. It don't have so much to do with brains as it does with common sense. And that's what you learn out here on the Slope. Horse sense. Ain't just anybody can fly one of those choppers."

I studied Will and read the pride in his face as he talked. I wondered if my father would ever speak so proudly about me. I wondered if I would ever mean as much to my dad as Billy meant to Will.

"Billy," Will said, shaking his head, "shucks, Billy didn't know any more than you did the first time he came out here. His mother wouldn't hardly let him out of her sight until he was your age. She didn't want him to be a cowboy like me. She wanted something more for him. Well, he crossed this Slope every spring for six years. And he turned into a mighty fine hand. Then he joined the service for a stint, and decided he wanted to be a pilot. He made it into flight school because he was smart, and he made it into choppers 'cause he wasn't only smart, he could think."

I thought about the wiry red calf I'd chased away from the herd that morning, and how a little thinking could have saved me a lot of embarrassment. Then I thought about how my good grades at school didn't count for anything out here on the Joshua Slope.

I swung the rope again, wound it up fast, and on the last swing dipped it over my left shoulder before I let it go, just like Will. The loop swished down smoothly around a cow's hind hocks. She stepped into the loop with her back legs. I pulled the slack and came up with two hooves on the line.

"That's it!" Will said. "We're gonna make a hand out of you yet."

It was close to two o'clock when I finally heard the rumble of Dad's truck behind us. He drove up slowly, with Buck standing black as night in the back and all our camping gear tied to the rack above the cab.

I was hungry.

Will pulled back from the herd and motioned for me to follow him. Dad stopped the truck and got out with the ice chest. Malcolm rode in from his position on the left wing, leaving the cattle on their own for a while. I asked Will if the cattle would be okay and he said not to worry. "They'll just stroll on up the road toward Shiloh Spring," Will said. "They can smell that summer pasture already. We'll catch up to 'em after lunch."

Will dismounted and got his horseshoeing equipment out of the truck. I watched him tack a new shoe on Roddy while Dad made more of the same old cold-cut–and–mayonnaise sandwiches. Malcolm pulled his saddle off Witch and tied her, ringing wet with sweat, to a tree. Everybody seemed to have something to do except me, until the sandwiches were ready. They tasted good because I was hungry, and because I was on the Joshua Slope and things just seemed to taste better out there. We were sweaty and tired and we all ended up sprawled under a big juniper tree, eating heartily and not talking. All you could hear were mouths chomping and the distant sound of cattle working their way up the country.

When we finished eating, Will got up and tapped me on the shoulder. He turned his head as though he wanted me to follow him. He walked bowlegged into the trees and I followed him like a sheep, wondering as we went what the old cowboy had in mind.

Soon we reached the edge of a small ravine, a steep drop-off where a steady stream of water fell into a beautiful little pool. The pool shimmered at the bottom, some twenty feet below us. A steep, rocky ledge surrounded most of the pool, except where the water spilled over a shelf and the stream continued southward. It was obvious no cows could get to the pool unless they were lowered on a rope.

Will gazed down at the water and smiled, then took off his dark glasses, looked over at me, and winked. I was startled by the deep blue of his eyes, blue as the pool below us, and the delicate white skin around his eyes where the glasses kept the sun from making it leather like the rest of his face. He put the glasses back on, hunched onto his hands and knees, and flopped his legs over the edge of the cliff. From there he worked his way down the ledge, finding steps here and there for footing. I watched him until he reached the bottom. At the edge of the pool he took off his hat and lay it on the grassy bank. Then he took off his shirt, his boots, his socks, and his pants. All he had on now were a pair of ancient-looking white briefs and his dark glasses. He looked up at me and with light glinting off his gold teeth said, "About time for a bath, wouldn't you say?"

I chuckled, but didn't answer. Will slipped his briefs off and stood there naked for a moment. He looked like a white marble statue. He was covered with black hair from his head to his ankles, but the skin beneath the hair was as white as the moonlilies we'd seen the day before. In spite of all the hair, it was the white that stood out most.

Will squatted and pulled a bandanna from the back pocket of his pants. Out of the cloth he unrolled a bar of soap. He waded into the pool until the water reached his waist. I could hear him shivering. He flipped water over his shoulders—taking short, panicked breaths—and lathered his chest with the soap.

It looked awfully refreshing. Still, I could not see myself naked in the pool.

Will finally took off his glasses and tossed them next to his clothes on the bank. Then he ducked his head underwater and quickly flipped it out, letting go a high-pitched bellow that bounded back and forth across the rocks. He soaped his hair, rinsed it, then looked up at me. "What's the matter? You bashful?" he said.

Of course I was bashful. The last thing I had imagined doing on the Joshua Slope was jumping naked into a pool with an old man. Then suddenly, without thinking, I slipped over the ledge and began climbing down to the pool. It was not me doing it. I didn't do things like that—not if I thought about them. I jumped off the last ledge onto the grassy bank and started to take my clothes off. Next to the pile of clothes I noticed Will's billfold. It had fallen out of his pants and lay open in the grass. All of his cards were tucked in plastic slots and I could see one clearly. It had Will's name typed boldly at the top: WILLIAM JOHN BUCHANAN. There was a picture of Will on the card, a photo that must have been taken many years before. It was Will, all right, but a much younger Will without a hat on, and with thicker, darker hair on his head. It was hard for me to think of Will as a young man. Yet there he was, young and smiling up at me. Then I heard his voice. "Hurry up," Will called. "We've gotta get back to the herd."

I threw off the rest of my clothes, all but my undershorts. My body was as white as Will's, but had very little hair. I couldn't bring myself to drop my shorts, so I waded in until my waist was covered, then took them off and threw them sloshing wet onto the bank.

The sharp water stole my breath. My tight, sore muscles drew up even tighter. Will handed me the soap and I washed the grime from behind my ears and the jam from between my toes. I washed all the sweat from me, all the dust of the Joshua Slope. I washed clean what was left of the dried blood on my injured arm, lathered the spot white where I had landed when Buck threw me. Dark red flakes fell softly to the water and floated slowly away.

When I had finished washing, Will waded over with a mischievous look on his face. He planted his huge, rough hand on my shoulder and, quick as a striking snake, pushed me into the water. I came up gasping, shivering, yelling, and tried to push Will, but he dodged me and I went under again. This time I came up laughing and Will started to laugh and we laughed together for a long time.

We finally got out and started dressing. Somehow it didn't bother me now to stand stark naked in front of Will. I looked up at the miniature waterfall that trickled into the pool. It seemed like a quiet miracle here in the desert, a small and simple blessing.

"Where does it come from?" I asked Will as we stood admiring the pool.

"From Shiloh Spring, five miles up," he said.

"Where does it go from here?"

"To Salt Pond," Will said. "Winds up in that

117

muddy little bog called Salt Pond down on the Slope. Hard to believe, ain't it?"

"Yes," I said, remembering the night I spent lost near Salt Pond.

We climbed up the ledge and walked back through the trees to the road. Will veered off toward Roddy, and I cut through a clump of junipers to where Justice was tied. Justice had eaten away all the shucks of grass around the pinion pine he was tied to. I led him back to the truck where Dad was waiting. Dad gave me a long, hard look as I approached and I wondered what I had done wrong now. Certainly it hadn't been wrong to go take a dip with Will.

"I'm gonna unload Buck," Dad said. "I want you to ride him again this afternoon."

A shiver ran through me as I looked up at Buck in the back of the truck. His profile was flat and dark, like a shadow cut from tin against the sky. I had hoped I would never have to ride him again.

"How about I finish the day on Justice?" I said.

"Buck needs to be used," Dad snapped. "He needs consistent use—now that we've got him started."

Now that I've *got him started,* I thought.

"He needs to be ridden every day if we're gonna make a horse out of him."

If I'm *going to make a horse out of him,* I thought.

"I'd really rather ride Justice," I said.

Dad tossed a bitter look at the ground. His jaw tightened and I could tell he was holding back a flash flood of anger. Just then Will rode up on Roddy. "Your father's right," Will said. "That colt needs some hard ridin' every day if you want to gain any ground on him. No need to get all hot and bothered. It'll be a piece of cake this time."

I looked up at Will, who had a big smile on his face. *Piece of cake?* Then I looked over at Dad, whose jaw was still stiff as rawhide. I turned my eyes back to Will and nodded. I'd do it for Will. Not for Dad, but for Will.

Dad backed the truck up to an embankment alongside the road. He unloaded Buck and I unsaddled Justice. I hefted the saddle up over Buck's arched back. I could tell by the way he humped his back he was feeling skittish. He was obviously loose and ready to fire. I dreaded the thought of climbing on him again. Slowly, one notch at a time, I snugged the cinch. I could feel him buzzing inside and he already gave off a hot, fuming smell. I pulled the cinch one more notch and Buck let out a long blow through his snotty muzzle. He sounded like a congested dragon.

I led Buck down the road a short way, trying to walk some of the play out of him. Then I walked him back to the truck and handed the reins to Dad while I snugged the cinch one more notch. Dad grabbed the reins close to the bit and twisted them into a tight bind so Buck would know who was boss. Once the cinch was set, Will rode up and grabbed Buck's headstall below the ear. He pulled Buck's head up against his thigh.

It was my move now. Time to get on. I was miserably uneasy and I tried once more to think of a way to weasel out, knowing full well that I had no choice now. I lifted my left leg and hopped just enough to poke my toe into the stirrup. Holding the reins and the saddle horn in my left hand, and the cantle of the saddle in my right, I pulled myself up and swung my right leg over Buck's rump. My undershorts were still wet from Shiloh Pool and I felt a little sloshy in the saddle. I evened the bridle reins, took a deep breath, and nodded for Will to let him go.

The second Will released Buck's head, the horse whirled, ducked, and came apart. He dropped his head so fast and so low the reins jerked out of my hands. I grabbed the saddle horn with both hands and held on with every string of strength in my body. Buck jumped and kicked and spun in a circle. It felt like the earth had fallen out from under me. Buck wanted me on the ground. But I didn't budge in the saddle. My wet pants were glued to the seat.

I had something to prove in those few seconds, though I didn't know exactly what. I had something to prove to Dad, to Will, to Buck—and to myself.

Buck kept after it. He twisted and folded and launched so far off the ground I saw the tops of the junipers. He squealed and snorted and even reached around with his teeth, his neck bent like a hairpin, and tried to bite my leg. With the reins gone, I had no control. I was helpless atop the exploding horse. I thought of ejecting like a fighter pilot, but I didn't have a parachute and it was a long way to the rocky ground. What's more, I knew that if I did go down, Buck's hooves would quickly be in my face—rocks below me and hooves above me. I was much safer on top of the horse than on the ground.

Buck finally slung back and reared, reaching high with his front hooves. The bridle reins fell into my lap. I grabbed them with one hand, still holding tight to the horn with the other. I jerked the reins and hauled the bit back into his mouth, letting out a yell that must have carried all the way down the Joshua Slope. I yanked on the reins with what little pride remained in me and pulled the spirit right out of Buck. A moment later he settled onto all fours. He locked his legs and stood stiff. Then he began to snuff at the ground, admitting defeat. I was in charge now, and Buck knew it. I looked over at Will and Dad through the settling dust and they knew it, too. Most important of all, *I* knew it.

Off in the trees I caught sight of Malcolm, who was anxious to catch back up with the herd. He sat atop Witch watching it all. He sat there for a long time, then nodded his head toward me, turned the mare, and trotted off.

Will rode up to me and smiled. "Call it your baptism of fire," he said, and he patted me on the shoulder.

Dad hobbled through the brush toward me and I thought I saw him wink at me. I thought I saw a twinkle in Dad's eye and a wink, and a kind of quick, proud smile. Whatever it was, it passed too quickly. While I was still trying to decide if it had all really happened, Dad looked at me sternly and said, "Don't let go of the reins next time."

18

We made another five miles that afternoon—good time considering some of the cows had grown sore-footed and slow. Buck ambled calmly up the road and didn't show a hint of fire the rest of the day. I could feel his defeat through the saddle.

By the time we got to Shiloh Spring Corral, it was early evening. Malcolm had ridden ahead with the hardy, fast part of the herd and left Will and me to bring up the slow bunch. Dad had gone ahead in the truck after lunch to make camp. When we got there, we corralled the cattle and threw fifty bales of hay over the fence to them. The hay had been stockpiled there earlier in the spring. Dad had a fire going, and the Dutch oven simmered.

I was hungry enough that night to eat horsemeat, but Dad had something better in mind. The smell of spuds sizzling in onions drew me like a magnet.

After taking care of Buck, I headed for the fire, straight for the food. Midway there I heard Will.

"How'd you like to help me, Brian?" he asked.

I turned toward him. He had Roddy tied to a tree and he held up a horseshoeing rasp.

I was going to ask him if I could eat first, but caught myself, remembering how Dad always said the animals come first. "Sure," I answered. I looked over at Dad by the fire, and realized he had been watching, waiting for my response. Then I turned back to Will. "I'd be glad to help you," I said, "if you'll tell me what to do."

"Ol' Roddy's about to lose his other hind shoe," Will said. "I've already put one shoe on today and the old back's about give out. Oh, you bet, I could do it if I had to. But I figure with a young back like yours in camp, no sense in an old man putting undue strain on his."

Dad had never asked me to help him shoe a horse.

I figured he was waiting until I got a little older, until I had a little more lead in my britches, since horseshoeing requires a great deal of strength as well as know-how.

Will showed me how to lift Roddy's hind leg and rest the hoof on my thigh. Then he talked me through the first steps of pulling the loose shoe off and running the rasp across the bottom of the horse's bare hoof until it was level and trim. My arms quickly grew weary.

"Billy could shoe a horse," Will said as he instructed me through the process. "He always shoed my horses."

I thought of Billy down on the border, Billy who crossed the Joshua Slope just like me when he was twelve. I wondered if he had felt the same things I did, if he had ridden up the road to Shiloh Spring in wet shorts like I had, if he had shoed his first horse on a quiet, beautiful evening just like this one.

Will was right. It was hard work putting the shoe on Roddy. It made my back ache, and my wrists and shoulders trembled under the strain. Little beads of sweat ran down my face, even though the evening air was cool. My injured arm still stung with pain, and my legs were sore from sticking to Buck that afternoon. Yet somehow all the pain felt good. It was the kind of pain that reminds you of what you've done and how far you've come.

One by one I pounded eight nails into Roddy's hoof to hold the shoe in place. Will showed me how to angle each nail just right—so it curved out the side of the hoof before it hit a nerve. He showed me how to twist the end of each nail and break it off even with the hoof, and how to tip each nail and file it smooth against the hoof's hard surface. It took me a long time, much longer than Will had taken to put the shoe on at lunchtime. My mouth watered as I thought of the potatoes all cooked and sitting warm in the pot near the fire.

When we were finished and Roddy stood level on his brand-new shoe, Will put his arm around my shoulder and squeezed it. I was sure he had done the same to Billy when Billy put on his first shoe.

In that silent moment as the sun ducked off the edge of the Joshua Slope, I felt as if Will wished I were Billy. And in that same moment as the evening was thick with the smell of fried spuds and onions, I wished that Will were my father.

19

◄◄◄◯►►►

I stayed at the fire for the stories that night. Will related how Roddy had turned right out of his shoe, the same shoe I had just stowed away for safekeeping in the bottom of my gear bag. He also talked of how well I'd handled Buck, how, instead of pitching out and giving up, I'd hung tight and finally gained control of the situation. The way Will told it made me sound like a hero or something. I sat there with a smile on my face and my chest full of pride.

It occurred to me as the evening drew long and the flames flickered low that I was part of them now.

Things had changed that much in one day. The night before I hadn't even felt worthy to sit at the fire, and now they were telling stories about *me*.

That night I dreamed a thousand things. They were crazy, jumbled dreams. Only one of the dreams remained clearly with me when I awoke.

I stood in the middle of a bare, lonely desert with nothing more than what was on my back. The mountain I struggled toward stood tall and blue on the horizon. Midway to the mountain I came upon a deep, narrow gash in the earth. I crept up to the edge, peered into the chasm, and discovered it went down forever. There was no way around; I had to cross it. The crack was only a few feet across, narrow enough that maybe I could jump it, but just far enough that I was left with some doubt. I looked around for a log or something to lay across the chasm. The desert floor was bare of everything but sand. Backtracking several steps, I readied myself to run and jump the deep hole. My heart began to leap in my chest and I could not build the courage to start. I walked to the edge and looked down again and measured in my mind the distance across.

Then I heard an odd noise in the sky. The sound

drew nearer. Fwap-fwap-fwap. *I looked up and saw a helicopter. The blades spun in a glimmering silver circle and the helicopter hovered directly above me, kicking up gray dust all around me. I heard a voice through a speaker from the chopper. "Try it," the voice said. "Get a good running start and try it. You can jump it. Lots of people have jumped it."*

I made frantic motions with my arms, trying to convince the pilot to land and give me a lift over the gully. Suddenly a rope dropped from the helicopter and the voice from the speaker said, "Tie the rope to your belt. I'm not allowed to carry you over, but I won't let you fall."

I tied the rope to my belt and moved back several steps from the chasm. The helicopter chopped the air above as I began my run. I hit top speed as I reached the edge, sprang from one foot, and sailed through the air. My toe caught the edge on the other side and I lunged forward into the hot sand and rolled to safety. The chopper landed and Billy got out. He ran over and patted me on the back. "You made it," he said. "You didn't even need the rope."

"Thanks," I said to Billy. He flashed me a huge smile that made me feel warm and peaceful, and we

129

talked for a long while about herding cows and chasing crazy calves and shoeing horses. Then he got back in the chopper and flew away.

And I woke up.

The sky was dark with clouds. Where there should have still been stars, there was only a gray-black blur. The clouds had rolled in thick and heavy, ready to burst like balloons. The moment I opened my eyes, I knew it was going to rain that day.

I could hear the cattle whining off in the distance—their sad, off-key bellows. I slid out of the warm covers, dropped my aching legs over the edge of the cot, and pulled on my cold Wranglers. From beneath the cot I grabbed my boots and tugged them on. My shoulders felt as if knives had been run through them during the night. A pain shot from my arms through my back and into my thighs and knees. Like a fire it ran the length of me and mixed and melted into one giant pain. I needed to walk it off. I slipped on my shirt, snaked into a pullover sweater, and wrestled into my denim jacket.

No one else was up yet.

I walked toward the corrals where the huddled cows and calves bawled in the early morning. Moving through the brush I was suddenly aware of a different sound. It was more a sigh—a low, bleating moan. I didn't hear it so much as I felt it. Fixing on the sound, I walked toward it.

The morning grew slightly lighter with each minute, still gray, but more distinct. I arrived at the corral and looked across the herd. Even then I could not zero in on the cow making the moaning noise. For a minute or so I studied the herd and listened.

Then I saw her.

The cow making the sad sound was on the far side of the corral, on the outside of the fence. She lay in a dreadful heap on the dewy ground.

I ran around the corral, stopping cold in my tracks a few feet in front of the cow. For a long time I stood frozen in the same position and studied her. I saw the *Flying-W* on her ribs. She was a young, white-faced crossbreed, one of Dad's prized replacement heifers. I groped toward her. Suddenly she swung her head over and looked up at me. I jumped back a step, my heart drumming. She stared at me with pleading eyes and made no attempt to get to her feet.

The cow's hind legs had been churning; they had cleared a smooth, clean opening in the brush. I thought she must be sick, and the awareness that she might be dying engulfed me. I started to turn, my first thought being that I should wake Dad so he could take over. Then I noticed a wet-looking bundle protruding from the cow's behind.

A peaceful feeling rippled over me now. It passed slowly and precisely through me, pushing the pain out the ends of my fingers, the tips of my toes, and the top of my head. I felt as if I were floating. I moved closer and studied the cow. She panted and gurgled and I was surprised at how she allowed me to approach.

Everything was fine. The cow was not dying, but exactly the opposite.

The cow was giving birth.

Maybe I should have called to Dad and the others. Instead, I squatted a few feet away and waited. The cow blathered and groaned and nothing happened.

I scooted nearer. The calf's head and front hooves were out. The slimy wet head and hooves had worked their way that far, but that was all. Nothing was happening, and it seemed that something should.

In an instant I felt peace turn to panic. Something *was* very wrong. The calf should have been out by now. Even *I* could see that. The calf should have been born and breathing by now.

I frantically searched the files in my brain for what I should do next. I had never seen it done, only heard the cowboys talk of it. "Pulling calves," Dad called it. Every spring Dad talked of pulling calves on first-time heifers when the calf was too big for the never-before mother. I thought of Dad again. I needed to wake him so he could handle the situation, but I had a strong feeling there was not time. What's more, I felt a new and wonderful sense of freedom. Without my father watching I felt free from his exacting standards, free to be capable.

My first impression had been true: The cow and calf were both dangerously close to death. I knelt down behind the struggling cow, remembering Will's words about Billy—that it's one thing to be smart, and something else to be able to think. Something had to be done quickly. I took hold of the calf's tiny front hooves. Its legs were warm and slick and difficult to hold on to. Gently I tugged. No movement. No give.

The calf was stuck at the shoulders. Half born, and stuck.

My heart raced as I realized how life existed here, now, but death lay very near. I dropped down on the cold ground and scooted up to the calf, drying my wet hands on my pants and taking another grip on the miniature front legs. I positioned my feet against the cow, pushed one boot against her hind legs and one against the top of her tail. Now I had some leverage. I could pull on the calf and push on the cow at the same time. Now I could make something happen.

The cow bellowed as I pulled. She moaned and cried and struggled.

I pulled.

Gripping the delicate little legs, I pulled with all my strength. I pulled the limp, warm, slick bundle of calf until it plopped out of the cow and fell into the world, until new life lay steaming and panting beside its mother. Then I fell back into the brush and caught my own breath.

When it was over, the sound of quiet startled me. Suddenly it was so quiet my ears felt the pressure. The silence was punctuated by the heaving of my chest.

Dawn had broken. There was light enough now to see off through the junipers and pinions and what few Joshuas remained now that we were starting up the mountain. The cows in the corral, the same cows that had bawled so horribly out of tune all night, now lined the fence, watching in silence. I had not realized it, but the cows had been watching the entire delivery.

As soon as I made eye contact with my audience, the cows broke ranks and fell away one by one. The spell dissolved and the silence ended and the cows began to mill and moo and everything was normal again.

Everything was normal except me.

Off in the gray distance I heard thunder roll down across the Joshua Slope. The thunder rumbled low and long, far away and soft.

Finally, I scooted away from the cow and her newborn calf and sat with my back against the rough trunk of a pinion pine. Then I heard my father's voice.

"Good work," he said.

The voice startled me. Dad had slipped up from behind. He stood beside me now, towering above me in his silver leg brace, and looked down with a smile. What he said and his pleasant look warmed me inside. I got up and stood next to him and we both noticed without actually saying it that I was taller than I used to be. I stood even with his shoulders.

"Good work," Dad said again. "We might have lost them both."

20

We rode out in rain that morning.

By the time we finished breakfast, saddled, and pushed the cattle out of the corrals, it was raining hard. Before we mounted, Dad pulled four yellow plastic slickers from behind the seat of the truck and handed one to me. I slid it over my head and let it fall all the way to my feet. It split below the waist so I could sit in the saddle and still not get my legs wet. It was fluorescent yellow, as were the others. We looked like cowboy firemen, bright flashing shapes in the dull morning, yellow men on horseback.

The rain fell in sheets and the slickers kept us dry.

Dad hummed through all of this. Rain, even the darkest rain, brightened my father's spirits. He came from a long line of dust-eating rain worshipers. Rain was a transforming thing for my father. It had a way of turning his mood. It did this by filling the ponds, replenishing the wells, settling the dust. It turned the dry bunchgrass green, brought on the June grass, the cicardy, and the Indian ricegrass. It transformed the dull gray hills into gleaming mounds of green. It did all the things my father hoped for and prayed for. And it made him hum.

I must have inherited my father's love for rain. The sound of thunder and the sight of curling gray clouds were always pleasing to me. The smell had a lot to do with it, the sharp scent of wet sage and dry earth turned damp, the pungent smell of wet juniper wafting from the branches. It was a kind of musty incense that fills the air and draws easily into you—the smell of everything's going to be okay.

As we lined the cattle out of the corral, Dad approached me with a bundle of brand-new calf in his arms. It was the same soggy little animal I had delivered that morning. "He's not in very good shape," Dad said. "It's a miracle he survived the birth. We could leave him and his mother here, but I'd rather bring them along so we can keep an eye on the little feller." Dad reached the calf up to me, hefted him over the saddle horn, up over Justice's tall withers, and lay him in my lap across the rain-soaked slicker. I would carry the calf in my lap the rest of the day, cradling him there with his mother laboring nervously alongside. Every hour or so I would stop and get off and let the calf suck from his mother. He would drink heartily and then we would go on in the driving rain, up the mucky, winding road from Shiloh Spring to Bunker Pass.

I rode behind the herd and kept the cattle moving through the rain. Will and Malcolm took the wings. They rode through the dark, stiff junipers and the lighter, fluffy pinion pines, their yellow slickers flicking like fire between the trees. I watched Will ride, the rain running like a waterfall off the brim of his hat and streaming down the back of his slicker onto Roddy's rump. Occasionally he would stop beneath a tall pine and let Roddy stand in the dry air for a moment. Then he would urge the horse on, talking softly to Roddy and cajoling him. He looked noble, Will did, like a brightly costumed knight astride the golden Roddy. He rode through the rain sitting straight in the saddle, his chin high so the water would run off the back of his hat.

On the other side of the herd Malcolm forced Witch through the trees like a slave driver; he kicked her and scolded her and pushed her through the dark forest. Malcolm hunkered in the saddle, his hat soaked to black, and bore down against the rain as if he were trying to duck it.

The newborn calf lay quiet and still in my lap. I felt his small, fragile heart thumping against my leg. His dainty pink eyelids squinted against the rain and he seemed to calmly accept this drenched new world. He seemed to accept it all without question. It was all he knew, I thought. He knew nothing of the hot, dry desert below us. So far he knew nothing more than rain and a steep, winding road up the mountain.

The Joshua Slope fell away behind us now. I looked back over my shoulder into the gray rain and considered how far we had come. Since my bath at Shiloh Pool and my run-in with Buck yesterday I was feeling much better about myself. The rain, though wet and uncomfortable, had brought with it a great deal of hope. There was also the calf in my lap. I felt proud that he was alive because of me. I began to feel that I had made it, that I had finished something.

Leaving the Slope behind and climbing the switch-backs up the mountain felt like the end of one thing and the beginning of another. Just as I began to re-lax with all these good feelings, Malcolm appeared alongside me. He rode quietly for a stretch, his eyes locked on the herd. A couple of times he seemed to want to start a conversation. Finally he grunted and said, "Long way to go yet." Then he spun away to the left and disappeared in the trees.

At noon Dad pulled up behind us. The truck tires plowed through the mud, leaving deep ruts. He stopped the truck in the middle of the road, got out, and began rigging up a lean-to tarp from the side of the stock racks. We ate lunch beneath the tarp while some of the cattle wandered on up the road. Most of them stopped, though, and spread into the trees to find shelter. From where I stood eating my sandwich I could see the sickly little newborn calf nuzzling close to his mother.

Dad was still jubilant. The rain possessed him like a silly spirit. "Ain't it beautiful?" he said. "Ain't it wonderful?" I ate my sandwich and smiled through all the happy talk.

Rain pelted the blue tarp as we ate. It came at a

strong and steady beat. Then, with no forewarning, it suddenly stopped. Just like that it quit.

All four of us stood beneath the tarp and listened to the surprising quiet. No one said anything. We ate and waited and listened. After a while we all took off our yellow slickers and hung them over the racks of the truck to dry.

Then we heard the sound. It came from far below on the Joshua Slope and began as nothing more than a faint rhythm. Not rain this time, but a constant, vibrating drone. The sound came out of the sky and floated slowly, persistently toward us.

We all looked at one another. Dad's face was a blank. Malcolm mumbled something. Will rubbed the black stubble on his chin. The sound drew nearer and the vibration became more distinct. It seemed to have homed in on us. We all stepped away from the truck and looked up into the gray sky. Nothing.

Yet the sound drew nearer.

I suppose I knew what it was before the others, even before any of us saw it. In the last moments before it appeared, I recognized the distinct *fwap-fwap-fwap*—the sound from my dream the night before. Just before it came into view, I knew.

A chopper had come for us.

"It can't be good," Malcolm moaned as the humming craft hung in the air above us.

"Unless it's Billy," I said.

I looked at Will, whose face was red with worry. "I certainly wasn't expecting him," Will said.

"Can't be good," Malcolm said.

The chopper floated down and landed on a wide and nearly level piece of road about fifty yards from us. Buck kicked and squealed in the back of Dad's truck. The other horses were tied far enough away that the chopper did not concern them. I walked out a few steps and stopped.

The chopper idled, its blades spinning slower and slower. No one got out. It was white with red letters on the door and it looked surprisingly small. The logo said AIR TIME AVIATION. There was just one man inside the clear bubble, and I heard Will mumble that he *wasn't* Billy.

Dad took charge and hobbled out toward the gyrating machine. I watched him in his leg brace limp out to the chopper so alien there in the junipers below Bunker Pass. Malcolm and Will stood by, dumbfounded. In all their years on the Slope they had never encountered such an unexpected visitor.

Hunching down, Dad hustled beneath the *fwap-*

ping blades. The pilot opened his door and spoke with Dad. Almost immediately Dad turned and looked at us. He pointed toward us and it seemed that he was pointing at Will. I could not read his expression.

Then Dad limped back toward us and Will started slowly out to him. They met midway between the chopper and the truck. Malcolm and I stayed put and watched as Dad reached his arm around Will's shoulders. They spoke with their faces unusually close as the chopper blades whirled slower and slower. We couldn't hear anything at all, could only watch their solemn discussion as the wind from the blades made their hat brims flap up and down.

All of a sudden Will's chin dropped. He took off his hat. His arms fell limp at his sides and he sank to his knees in the mud. He stayed on his knees for a long time, his head turning from side to side as if he were saying no. Dad finally helped Will up and accompanied him to the chopper, walking slowly with his arm around Will's shoulders.

My heart had settled like a rock at the bottom of my stomach, and now my throat swelled up as I watched Will climb through the chopper door, into the transparent bubble, and buckle into his seat.

From fifty yards away I could see him in his seat with his hat on his lap and his thin hair matted down where the hatband had pressed. From fifty yards I could tell that Malcolm had been right and that none of this was good.

The chopper lifted slowly, rose above the trees, and hovered for a short, somber moment above us. Then it fell away into the sky and disappeared through the clouds.

Dad watched until it was gone. After a long stretch of time he turned and limped heavily back to us. When he reached the truck, he leaned against the red racks and took off his hat.

"It's Billy," Dad said. "He was on a search-and-rescue mission last night. Got caught in a storm—must have been the same one that hit us this morning." Dad stopped for a moment, ran the sleeve of his shirt across his eyes, and cleared his throat. "High winds. Poor visibility. The helicopter went down. Billy was killed instantly."

Silence.

Finally Dad finished his report. "Will's wife didn't get word until early this morning. She needs him home."

I could see a mist in Dad's eyes. I'd never seen him

cry before. Malcolm wandered off into the wet trees and kept his back to us as he lit a cigarette and puffed the smoke up toward the treetops. I lifted my arm, covered my eyes, and sobbed into my shirt-sleeve.

After a while I stopped sobbing and listened to the steady *drip-drop-drip-drop* from the moist tree branches. It seemed the whole mountain was crying. Trailing white clouds rolled slowly up from the Slope and over the top of the ridge. I stood alone on the road and listened.

Dad appeared next to me. He put his arm around my shoulders, just as he had put it around Will's, and squeezed me hard. He held me the way a father who is grateful to have his son beside him does.

I thought for a moment that I could hear the drone of the helicopter, faint and fading in the distance.

21

The rain did not return that day. By midafternoon the sun was out and all of Clover Mountain sparkled like crystal. Malcolm and I drove the cattle on up the mountain road. We each took a wing and dropped into the center occasionally to keep the stragglers moving. Dad drove ahead in the truck, pulled right up through the herd with Buck and Roddy in the back. It must have seemed odd to Roddy, being in the middle of everything one minute, and suddenly abandoned the next. I choked hard to keep from crying again as Dad passed us and pulled up through the herd with Roddy.

We were nearly to the top of the mountain now. A fresh, moist breeze blew through Bunker Pass and snaked down over us. We were working our way into the larger pines and I could see a few tall, majestic ponderosas on the ridge. Once, as the road steepened for the last climb to Bunker Pass, I stopped Justice and turned him back toward the south. From there I could see the entire Joshua Slope. I gazed down across the rolling desert, over the hills and humps and hollows. Far off against the clean new sky I saw Signal Peak. It looked just like it had looked the day I was lost, only much farther away. I thought how I no longer needed that landmark, not now that I was nearly to the top of Clover Mountain. Up here I would have to find new landmarks. I sat for a long time looking over the country below. It was dotted with hundreds, thousands, maybe millions of Joshua trees. Each tree stood firm against the wind, each one with twisted arms pointing the way. Thousands of them, maybe millions—each one separate and different with a story of its own.

We made Bunker Pass Corral well before sundown. The baby calf was asleep in my lap. I stroked his soft new hide one last time before I handed him down to Dad. Though the calf was small and light, my legs felt like an enormous weight had been lifted from them. The calf seemed to be doing well, taking nourishment from his mother and able to wobble around on his knobby little toothpick legs. Still, Dad figured I ought to carry him the rest of the way to the valley tomorrow. I didn't mind the assignment at all.

It was quiet in camp that night. Sitting on a juniper stump next to the fire, I had a feeling that this might someday become the most-told story of all. But not tonight. It would take time to become a story. Tonight it was nothing more than a hollow feeling.

The next morning we got up early for the last push to the valley. I figured I'd be riding Buck again and I didn't have a problem with that. I wasn't afraid of Buck anymore, not now that I knew how to show him who was boss. If Dad wanted me to ride Buck, I was ready. In fact, I was a little disappointed when he finally decided to have me saddle Justice. He wanted me to carry the weak calf again, and he figured things would go a lot better on Justice.

We drove the tired herd across the green mountain flats, plodding slowly through pastures of cheatgrass and wildflowers. The flowers had bloomed like a miracle—yellow, blue, and red. They carpeted the clearings with astonishing color.

It was noon when we finally topped the ridge above the valley. As we rode to the edge, the broad, long fields of timothy grass suddenly appeared below us—the lush, beautiful pastures where the cows would summer.

"Quite a sight," Malcolm said as he rode up beside me. "I remember *my* first time like it was yesterday. We'd been down on that desert gathering cows for a dreadful week and when we finally made it to here, I thought we'd reached the promised land."

I smiled at Malcolm, but he took off before I could say anything. I watched as he and Witch ambled down the road and wondered if I'd ever figure him out. For a long time I sat there on Justice with the baby calf in my lap and admired the scene. Before me lay the valley that belonged to my father and not to the government, the meadowlands where my great-great-grandfather had settled among the Indians and built a home of lumber harvested from these very trees. I recognized it all because I'd spent two weeks in this valley every summer since I could remember. But we had always come in on the road from the north. This was my first approach from the south over the Joshua Slope.

The cattle streamed down the road and into the valley like water running back to the sea. They were tired, ragged, and sore-footed, but as soon as they caught sight of the meadows, the moment they smelled the thick, wet grass below, they began to jump and kick and trot down the road with new life.

I lifted the baby calf's chin and showed him his summer home. "This is it," I told him. He didn't seem impressed at all. Malcolm had stopped along the road and gotten off. He was waiting for us. When we got to him, I hefted the calf down into Malcolm's arms and he set the quivering little thing gently onto its feet. The calf listed away on tenuous legs toward his mother.

"We're back again," Malcolm announced. He heaved a long, rough sigh. Then he took off his hat and rubbed his lips across the sleeve of his shirt. "Prettiest sight of the year."

I'd been thinking of Will all day—about where he was and what he was feeling and how I wished that he were here. I was finally over the Joshua Slope, had made it all the way across. This was a moment I had looked forward to celebrating; and I had planned on celebrating it with Will, not with Malcolm. Now that it was here, I didn't feel like celebrating at all. Now all I felt was emptiness.

Malcolm swung back onto Witch and mumbled what a shame it was about Billy. We continued down the winding road to the valley.

That night we stayed in the pine-board house my great-great-grandfather built more than a hundred years ago. The warped and weathered house stood small and humble among a grove of towering cottonwood trees. I slept in a squeaky wrought iron bed between a pile of musty handmade quilts with the window open and the night breeze streaming through the cottonwood leaves.

I went to sleep with thoughts of Will, and with a deep, heavy sadness. Yet somewhere inside me a good feeling was trying to break through, a feeling of satisfaction about the job completed. The next morning, however, I awoke to learn that there was still plenty to do, that the real work was only just beginning. We spent the entire day in a complex of big, dusty corrals near the house. It was sorting time now, which meant we must separate all the cows and calves into three corrals—one for Dad, one for Malcolm, and one for Will.

Immediately after breakfast we crossed the lane to the corrals and went to work. I manned one gate, Malcolm another. Dad brought a bunch of cattle into a long alleyway and began to study them. He seemed happy that we'd finally reached this part, something he could be physically involved in, because it was all done on foot and didn't require him to straddle a horse. He studied the cattle until he determined which calf belonged to which cow, then hobbled in with his buggy whip and cut a pair away from the rest. As he ran them down the alleyway, he called out, "Malcolm," "Will," or "Mine." If the cow and calf were Will's, I opened my gate and let them into my corral. If they were Malcolm's, he opened his gate. If the pair belonged to my father, Dad pulled a side gate open and pushed them into yet another corral.

This went on all day, Malcolm occasionally changing places with Dad. I watched them intently and tried to figure out how they paired the cows and calves. It was mostly color, I thought. They could tell by looking at the color and markings of the cow and

152

calf. But as the day wore on, and new layers of dust caked on my sweaty arms and neck, I realized that Dad and Malcolm depended on much more subtle evidence to determine the pairs. Color was part of it, but so was the shape of the calf's face and the way it acted and moved, and, most importantly, the way the cow and calf interacted with each other. I began to notice how a cow would keep a corner of her eye on her own calf, and how a calf, in spite of all the traffic and confusion, always knew where its mother was. Once in a while you actually saw a calf sucking from its mother, which clinched it right there. Usually you had to go on less solid evidence.

I was amazed at how Dad and Malcolm did it. They were absolutely certain of each pair they sent down the alley, knew without doubt the two belonged together, and knew instantly which corral they should go into. For me it was much more difficult than any test I'd ever taken at school. Concentrating on each decision made my head ache.

Once in a while I would think of Will and my chest would tie up in knots. But you couldn't let your mind wander when you were cutting cattle, and I was grateful to be so busy. Dad and Malcolm seemed to have put Will and Billy out of their thoughts. Yet, once, as Dad drove a cow and calf of Will's down the alley, and Malcolm watched me swing the gate shut behind them, I detected a woeful look on both of their faces.

After lunch Dad started bringing cattle down the alley much faster. A couple of times I got caught with my mind somewhere else and missed my gate swing. Dad frowned at me the few times I messed up, but for the most part he seemed pleased with my performance. I made myself settle in and keep focused on the job, and after that I didn't miss another gate swing. By midafternoon I felt ready to try a stint at the other end of the alley. "Hey," I yelled as Dad limped up the lane for another pair. "Let me try it."

Dad turned and shot me a sour glance. His dust-caked face looked like a Halloween mask. The message in his eyes seemed to be that I had no business asking for such an important job.

Malcolm spoke from behind. "Give the boy a shot," he said. "You could use a break."

I turned and looked at Malcolm. There was a hint of a smile on his face, enough so that I could finally imagine what a real Malcolm Higginbotham smile would look like. He lifted his chin toward the cows and calves at the end of the alley. "Go git 'em," he said.

I walked up to Dad. He started to hand me the buggy whip. Then he paused and drew it back. I reached and grabbed the whip—took it right out of Dad's hand—and headed for the cattle.

The first pair was easy. I'd noticed the calf nursing from its mother a few minutes earlier, and also the *Rocking-B* on the cow's left shoulder. I cut the cow and calf apart from the rest and sent them down the alley. "Will's," I yelled.

Next I zeroed in on a red bolly cow whose calf could have been one of several little critters dancing nearby in the dust. I studied the cow, noticed the *M-Bar-H* on her left ribs, and made a mental note that she was Malcolm's. Now I had to be patient. I could not afford to make a hasty decision. I had to watch and study and process every piece of information. The cow looked around at one particular calf. He was a bolly calf—black bolly instead of red. There were two red bolly calves near the black. Either of the reds seemed a much more likely candidate, but the red cow was watching the black calf. I remembered Malcolm's black Angus bull among the herd sires we had brought over the Slope. Maybe the Angus bull was the father and that was why the red cow had a black calf. I had to be more than smart now; I had to think. The cow kept an eye glued on the little black bolly. I watched closely for another clue. Suddenly the cow sent a low, raspy moan through the dust. I heard the black calf's soft, gurgling reply and locked in my decision. I sent the unlikely pair down the lane and yelled, "Malcolm's." Then waited for a response.

Malcolm routinely opened his gate and let the pair in. He said nothing. Dad said nothing. Their silence confirmed it. I was right!

My heart swelled. I had never felt quite this proud of myself. I wanted to celebrate someway, but there were a lot more cows and calves to separate and the two tired cowboys at the gates didn't seem at all festive.

I hustled back to the top of the alley and cut out an easy pair of Dad's. Running them down the alleyway, I hollered, "Yours."

Dad opened the gate and as the cow and calf burst into the corral, I swear I heard him say, "Ours."

Ben Walker, our neighbor from town, came to the ranch in his pickup that night. He brought word that Billy Buchanan's funeral would be the next day. Dad and Malcolm talked at length about it, finally deciding that Dad would drive the truck to town the next morning and represent the three of us at the service. Someone would have to stay with the cattle, and Malcolm was the natural choice. "Next funeral I go to'll be my own," he muttered. "I'll pay my respects to Billy right here in the wide open. This valley is my chapel."

Deep down I wanted to go to town with Dad, wanted to see Will and shake his hand or pat him on the shoulder, or do something to show him I cared. But Dad thought I should stay with Malcolm and help him get started with the branding. And I figured Will would probably be glad to know that I was helping hold down the fort while he was gone.

Malcolm and I spent the next day branding, castrating, and earmarking calves. We vaccinated every one, gave them shots against blackleg, the scours, pneumonia, and brain fever. It was the hardest work I'd ever done. An endless line of calves moved one by one through the chute and the sun beat down like a club. My clothes dripped with sweat, and dust clung to my skin until it became mud.

By nightfall Dad was back. He went straight to the kitchen and fixed our supper. I dragged into the house and devoured the thick stew full of fresh vegetables he had cooked. He didn't have much to say about the funeral, only that it was a fine service and that Will and his wife seemed to be holding up well considering the circumstances. I went to bed and slept soundly until Dad's big hand shook my shoulder before light in the morning.

We did the same thing all the next day.

There was no joy or glory in any of it. None of this was what I had expected it to be, although I kept thinking that it might have been if the chopper had not dropped in that day.

More than anything I missed Will. I thought of him as the hours passed, as we ran the calves through the squeeze chute, one at a time, and pressed the searing irons into their quivering ribs, and smelled the pungent smoke as it curled off the burning hide—the strangely satisfying smell of burnt flesh as we branded an endless line of calves. Each time one of Will's calves came in, they handed the iron to me and I stamped Will's big *Rocking-B* on the bellowing calf's left shoulder.

22

There was a bright slice of moon the night before we went home. It was a silver-black night in early June. I lay sleepless on the quilts, listening to my dad snore. In the next room Malcolm Higginbotham hacked and wheezed and coughed. Old Malcolm may have never gone to sleep that night. It was as if he had to purge his lungs of fifty years' worth of cigarette smoke before he could rest.

Lying wide-eyed on the quilts, I watched the dusty moonlight stream in through the open windows. Looking up at the hundred-year-old planks on the ceiling, I could see toolmarks in the wood and I marveled at the thought that they had been made by my great-great-grandfather's plane. A thousand thoughts swirled in my mind. It was Will I thought of most, how he had become my friend in such a short time, how he had helped me over the Slope, and how he didn't deserve to suffer the way he must be suffering.

I thought of home and of Mom and of Michael Bonner and Christy Harris. But it was Will I thought of most.

It had been a long time since I'd heard any music, days since I'd felt the beat of anything beyond the pounding of an animal's heart.

A thought had occurred to me as we pushed the herd over the Slope: that I might be able to pick up Rockin' Robby on the cattle truck radio. Near midnight, knowing sleep was still off in the distance, I decided to give it a try. I slipped out of bed with nothing more than gray moonlight in the room. I pulled on my pants and a jacket and stepped into my boots.

It was just a few steps through the cool night air to the truck. I climbed into the cab and sat behind the wheel. Dad always left the keys in the ignition so they'd be where he wanted them when he needed them. Turning the key one click lit the dashboard, then I switched on the radio.

Static.

There was nothing but fuzzy noise up and down the dial. Slowly and anxiously I turned the tuning knob, rolled it from one end of the dial to the other. At certain spots I caught a hint of music—wishful thinking more than anything.

Minutes later, maybe the full eternity of ten minutes, I finally hit on something more than static. I fine-tuned the dial, turned it with the precision of a surgeon, until the voices became crisp.

Suddenly the talking stopped and there was music. In the middle of a silver night on Clover Mountain, sitting behind the wheel of my dad's cattle truck, I finally heard music again. The signal strengthened and I felt the chords and the beat.

A sudden giddy joy overcame me. I made a fist and pounded it on my leg and yelled, "Yes!" so loud the men inside the house could have easily heard me. It was wonderful to hear the music again. I thought of the night before I left and how I stayed up most of it at Michael Bonner's house, listening to every CD the two of us owned.

The song was long and it pounded heavily into the night. My shoulders ached and my battered legs felt constricted in the cab of the truck. I thought of all the work that had to be finished tomorrow, and how much more time meant to me now, especially time to sleep. The music sounded good, though—too good—and I couldn't let go. I lay my head back on the seat and smiled into the darkness until I finally dozed off.

I don't know how long I slept, but when I awoke, the music had disintegrated into static. I clicked the key to the off position and sat for a precious few moments in the quiet, then softly slipped back into the house, pulled off my clothes, and went to sleep between the quilts.

23

It was still dark when I awoke. Dad and Malcolm were in the kitchen sipping coffee. I could hear them talking above the sizzle of bacon and eggs. I woke up to the aroma of comfort and contentment that came rolling in from the kitchen. Dad and Malcolm were in a deep discussion. I lay between the warm quilts and listened.

"He might make a hand after all, Dad said."

"I'll tell you one thing," Malcolm said, "he earned his salt the day you were gone." Malcolm's voice was raspy and he coughed once or twice between every sentence. "Count yourself lucky he's here and not out roaming the streets."

It finally sank in that they were talking about me.

"I wish he'd get a decent haircut," Dad said.

"There's lots worse things," Malcolm replied.

The house fell quiet for a moment.

I hung on the edge of the silence, straining to hear more. Finally I heard my father's voice again. He spoke in a low, somber tone that sounded foreign to me. "I was never so worried in my life as that night Brian was lost."

I sat up suddenly in bed and positioned myself to hear everything. They were talking quietly and must have assumed I was still asleep, but I could hear them well enough, and though it frightened me that I might hear something I didn't want to hear, I listened anyway.

"Gettin' lost, hell, that's just part of growing up," Malcolm said. "Wasn't that long ago you were a kid yourself, Jake. Remember that time you got lost down in Dodge Wash? You wouldn't have been any older than Brian then. Your pa was raving mad when you didn't get back to camp on time. We went out looking for you and I was the one that found you, right after sundown, sittin' up next to a Joshua tree, head buried in your arms, cryin' up a storm."

I heard my father chuckle. "The thing I remember most about that night was how you cheered me up," Dad said. "You started telling me all those sappy stories about how tough it was when *you* were a kid. How you tended those sheep alone for weeks at a time out on Black Rock. You put me back on my horse and talked me out of my crying and by the time we got to camp I felt just fine."

"Yes sir," Malcolm said. "I never did tell your father what a boob you were out there. And you've stuck to me like glue ever since."

Dawn began to break. Dull, early light filtered into the room. I sat in bed with a smile on my face and listened to more of their talk.

"I was awful lucky to have you around," Dad said to Malcolm. "My dad rode me hard when I was a kid. I never felt like I measured up." Dad paused for a moment, probably taking a bite of breakfast. "I suppose Brian feels the same way. I never realized how hard it is to get a boy across that Slope the first time. It's good Will was there to take him under his wing."

"Just like *you* were there to take Billy under yours," Malcolm said. "Ol' Will was every bit as hard on Billy as you've been on Brian."

165

I started to choke up when they mentioned Will and Billy. Apparently Dad and Malcolm were stunned themselves when the names were voiced. They stopped talking, and there was a kind of unofficial moment of silence.

Then Malcolm spoke again. "Every boy ought to have a man for a friend," he said. "A boy should count himself lucky if he's got one, and blessed if it happens to be his father." Malcolm coughed and I heard him spit in the sink. I remembered what Will had said about Malcolm's father leaving when he was just a boy. Then I remembered what Malcolm had said about riding with old Josh Whitaker. Maybe Josh had been there for Malcolm just like Will had been there for me.

The bunkroom grew brighter with morning light. I laced my fingers behind my head and sank back into the soft pillow. *If I ever have a son,* I thought, *I'll be both father and friend.* Then I pictured Dad sitting in the kitchen with his knee brace on, remembering with Malcolm, recalling the first time *he* crossed the Slope. It must not have been easy for him to bring me out here and let me make all those mistakes.

"I'm proud of the boy," Dad finally said.

* * *

After that, Dad and Malcolm must have both realized they were getting a little deep into things they weren't comfortable talking about. Malcolm suddenly changed the subject to the current price of hay. That was my cue. I was supposed to feed the cattle in the corrals before breakfast. I got up, put on my stiff clothes, and headed toward the kitchen to say good morning. Crossing through the parlor between the bunkroom and the kitchen, I changed my mind and quickly stepped out the front door. I wasn't in the right frame of mind just then to wander in and join their talk. I hurried over to the corrals and did the feeding. Then I started down the lane toward the timothy meadow.

At the horse barn I stopped and grabbed a nose bag and a halter and went into the dark feed shed. The air inside was thick with grain dust. I held my breath, filled the bag with oats, and continued down the lane to the meadow.

At the gate I stopped and looked across the dew-glazed grass. A flock of blackbirds swooped down and chirped low over the timothy. The horses grazed at the far end of the meadow, two hundred yards away.

I whistled. The horses' heads lifted in unison. I raised the nose bag and shook it. Suddenly the horses whirled and mounted a charge toward me. I climbed over the gate and moved toward them, shaking the bag of oats as I walked. The horses quickly drew nearer and soon I recognized the features of each one: Justice in the lead, his red mane flying in the bright morning. Behind him ran Buck, black as tar, and Witch, who looked beautiful at full stride, head and all. I looked for Will's golden Roddy, but he was not running with the rest of them.

Soon I caught sight of Roddy up in a far corner of the meadow. He stood alone, grazing slowly on timothy grass.

Roddy was the one I wanted. I poured the grain out on the ground and dropped the nose bag. The horses rumbled up to me, slid in the moist grass, and stopped. It wasn't me they were running to. It was the grain. I left it for them and walked off toward Roddy, up through the meadow with the halter.

He did not move as I approached. I walked up to him slowly and talked softly, said quiet things like "whoa, boy, easy, boy, easy now."

Roddy didn't seem to care whether I caught him or not. I slipped the halter on, buckled it, and led him back to the gate. At the barn I tied him to a post and curried him. I brushed him long and hard, gave him a thorough going-over. I started to pull my saddle out of the shed, then noticed Will's on a stand over in the corner. I put mine back and pulled Will's saddle out. I put Will's pads and saddle on Roddy, then replaced the halter with a bridle and climbed on. Will's stirrups fit me perfectly. I smiled at the thought of Will's stirrups fitting me.

I nudged Roddy with the heels of my boots and we headed straight into the morning.

It was five miles back to Bunker Pass at the edge of Clover Mountain. Roddy clipped along at a steady pace, smooth and constant and true. I knew it was irresponsible to ride off like that, without letting anyone know. It was something I had to do, though— something I could never explain to Dad—so I rode on, in spite of the little needle of guilt that jabbed at me along the way.

We were going back, Roddy and I. Back to the edge of the Slope. I wished that we could go all the way to the beginning and start it over again, but I knew we could only go to the edge. You could never go all the way back. You could cross the Slope again and again, but you could only cross it once for the first time.

It took us an hour to reach the pass. Roddy stopped beside a towering ponderosa pine. A breeze streamed up from the desert and rolled waves across the cheatgrass. The pine tree rocked and creaked like an antique clock. I took off my hat and felt the cool air through my hair. Roddy's golden mane lifted and fluttered in the wind.

The mountain dropped here, fell fast and steep and sloped off into desert. The low gray ridges in the distance folded over their own shadows in the morning sun. Across the long reach of country I saw countless dots, which I knew were Joshua trees.

Roddy stood silent in the breeze and I listened to the rocking pine tick away time.

All of a sudden Roddy cranked his head to the left and pricked his ears toward something. I sighted between his ears and saw what he saw—a cow and calf huffing up the road toward Bunker Pass. They were coming on their own, a tired bolly-faced cow and a slick red calf, trailing up the mountain of their own free will.

As I watched the pair make their way up the steep grade, I began to wonder. I asked myself why it was necessary to do all of this. It seemed that eventually all the cattle would have worked their way over the

Slope on their own. They would have followed the natural map in the landscape of their minds, would have found the winding road and climbed to summer pasture without anybody's help.

Why couldn't we have just let them come on their own? We could have waited for them and gathered them when they got here, could have branded and doctored and separated them once they'd made their own way up the Slope. I could have stayed home and gone to school and listened to my CDs and hung out at Michael Bonner's house. I could have danced with Christy Harris at the School's Out dance and cruised Main all night with the freshmen and slept in my warm, soft bed. I could have done all that and never bothered with the Joshua Slope.

Maybe it doesn't work if you don't give them a push, I thought. Everything needs a push now and then. Cows and people, both.

The cow and calf crested the ridge and picked up speed as they passed just a few yards away. Through a break in the trees I saw a *Rocking-B* brand on the cow's left shoulder. She belonged to Will. I studied the calf as it tagged close to its mother and realized how much more I saw now—things I would have never seen before. I didn't just see a calf; I saw a female calf, a well-built heifer, long across the back and deep in the chest and hindquarters. I saw what Will would have seen—a fine replacement heifer.

But there was something else I detected as the calf trotted through the trees, something that suddenly turned me numb all over. It was the way the calf craned her tail in the air, the extra spring in her legs, the flaring mischief in her eyes. She had to be, *definitely was*, the same red devil I had chased into the desert a few days before. The same calf Will and Roddy had handled so smoothly, the one that had caused me to act without thinking and left me feeling like a fool in front of Will.

The calf had come back, just as Will had assured me she would.

I settled deep in the saddle and smiled into the sun, knowing now that it had all become a story.

With a flick of the reins I turned my back on the Joshua Slope. Roddy took it from there. We followed the cow and calf to the valley, all the way back to the meadows and breakfast.